"The Magic—It's As Real As We Are,"

James said huskily, touching his lips to Caroline's throat.

Her senses whirled, but she managed to ask, "How can you be so certain?"

His smile held indulgence, as well as pleasure. "Because I believe in it, with everything I am or hope to be."

With a sigh, Caroline linked her hands together behind his neck and gazed into his eyes. "Teach me to believe, James."

"We'll teach each other," he promised. "And whatever you do, don't let these feelings frighten you."

Any apprehension Caroline had was eased by his words. "I'm not afraid of you, only of what's happening to me."

He met the forest-green depths of her eyes and whispered. "It's happening to both of us, darling."

"We barely know each other, and yet we..."

"We what?"

"We burn together...."

Dear Reader:

Six down, six to go... It's July, and I hope you've been enjoying our "Year of the Man." From January to December, 1989 is a twelve-month extravaganza at Silhouette Desire. We're spotlighting one book each month with special cover treatment as a tribute to the Silhouette Desire hero—our *Man of the Month*!

Created by your favorite authors, these men are utterly irresistible. One of Lass Small's Lambert sisters gets a very special man in July. *Man of the Month* Graham Rawlins may start as the *Odd Man Out*, but that doesn't last long....

And Mr. August, Joyce Thies's *Mountain Man* thinks he's conquered it all by facing Alaska, America's last frontier—but he hasn't met his mail-order bride yet!

Yours,

Isabel Swift
Senior Editor & Editorial Coordinator

NOELLE BERRY McCUE
Magic Touch

Silhouette Desire

Published by Silhouette Books New York

America's Publisher of Contemporary Romance

SILHOUETTE BOOKS
300 East 42nd St., New York, N.Y. 10017

ISBN: 0-373-05510-2

First Silhouette Books printing July 1989

NOELLE BERRY McCUE,

who helped launch the Silhouette Desire line under the pseudonym Nicole Monet, lives in California with her literary agent husband, Ric, and their daughter, Katie. "I've always loved to read," the author says, "and writing has filled a void in me I was never consciously aware of having. It has added depth to my life, and a greater awareness and appreciation of the people around me. With every book I write, I hope I am in some small way paying for the pleasure reading has given me over the years. If I can help just one person find enjoyment and release from everyday troubles, then I've accomplished my purpose in my chosen field."

The author concludes by saying, "That's why I write romances, because they leave the reader with a positive attitude toward love, life and relationships. When all is said and done, isn't it love for others that gives us the greatest happiness in life?"

One

Caroline Barclay glanced at the digital clock radio on the nightstand. Six thirty-three in the evening, she thought, and all is definitely not well. She had followed her husband into their bedroom at his request, watched unsuspectingly as he closed the door on their teenage son, and spent the following half hour listening to the sound of his voice. Now...she was watching him pack.

"Did you hear what I said, Caro?"

She nodded, leaning forward until she was perched on the edge of the bed they had shared for nearly twenty years. She fought against hysterical laughter when she realized that "perch" was a very good word for what she was doing. She reminded herself of a pouter pigeon poised and ready for flight, her feathers ruffled in indignation.

Right now she would like nothing more than to soar away into the sky; to find freedom from the earthly ties that bound her. If she had the choice she would be an eagle, strong, proud and fearless. Unfortunately she had no choice, no pride, and certainly no strength. Her usually delicately arched brows furrowed in concentration as she struggled to control the emotions threatening to rip away her dignity. If she *were* an eagle soaring into the sun, she would pause in flight only long enough to do a number on Frank's head, she decided.

Her hands were shaking as she clutched at the side of the mattress. It had a familiar, welcoming feel, and she grabbed hold in desperation. She remembered her excitement when she and Frank had begun furnishing their first tiny apartment prior to their wedding. Her mouth curved in a tiny moue of recollection. She had wanted comfort, but he had insisted that the hard, orthopedically correct monstrosity they finally bought would last through their years together. She had deferred to his judgment, an error repeated with habitual regularity as the years passed. But Frank had certainly been correct in his assessment, she admitted grudgingly, her knuckles whitening as her grip tightened. The mattress was in great condition. It was their marriage that had fallen apart.

"Damn it, Caro," Frank shouted, turning away from the closet with a bunch of shirts over his arm.

"The problem's not going to go away because you refuse to acknowledge it."

"Until tonight I wasn't aware there was a problem."

God, she hated her voice! She sounded hesitant, timid, when all she really wanted to do was rake her nails down the side of his good-looking face. Blond and blue-eyed, the round-cheeked "baby face" that had long been the bane of his existence had certainly stood him in good stead. Frank was handsomer now at forty-three than he'd been on their wedding day. His stomach didn't look like a road map because of the stretch marks earned by carrying his child, nor had his stocky frame blurred with excess poundage as he approached middle age.

No housewife syndrome for Frank! He played tennis and swam at his club three days a week, while the only exercise she managed was pushing a vacuum cleaner and running around the supermarket. As a young wife actively involved in the daily activities of her son, she'd never visualized the loneliness in store for her as the mother of a popular teenager. She'd expected her relationship with her husband to grow and deepen as the years passed and Peter grew up, so the reality had been something of a shock. As a result, during the last few years of Pete's maturing independence her body had blossomed forth in glorious protest to the consoling tidbits she'd chomped on while Frank "worked late" at the office.

When Pete was younger he had worked wonders for her waistline, but now that he was a senior in high school he was busy with football, girls, and his part-time job at the local hamburger joint. Although she was proud of his popularity and thoroughly approved his independence, Caroline would have been the first to admit that at times she missed being a part of car pools, Little League practice, PTA meetings, and the hundred and one daily chores that went with parenting a healthy, grubby little boy.

"If there was no problem, I wouldn't be asking you for a divorce, would I?"

Caroline transferred her hands to her lap, and began to pluck at the tiny balls of fur embedded in her polyester slacks. The pants were wrinkle free, which cut down on her ironing. They had a stretch waistband, which aided her breathing. The manufacturer had never mentioned fur balls. She noticed the spread of her thighs against the material, and self-consciously went on tiptoe to alleviate the pressure.

Lifting her head, she caught sight of her reflection in the dressing-table mirror. Her shoulders were slumped, their plump outline a caricature of feminine perfection. Tonight her whole life had become a caricature, she thought, a mockery of what she had always imagined it to be. She straightened her back, as though the mute defiance in the gesture could free her from the nightmare Frank had plunged her into with such callous suddenness.

Nervously she tugged at the buttoned collar of her white blouse, the tightening muscles in her throat threatening to choke her. "What in God's name am I going to tell Peter?"

Frank turned at her distraught whisper, his thin-lipped mouth curving in disgust. "That's all this means to you, isn't it?"

He gestured toward the suitcase open at the foot of the bed and the clothes piled high beside it. "You don't give a damn that I'm leaving you. All you can think of is what people will say."

"I don't give a tinker's damn about the conjectures of our family and friends," she insisted in a voice clipped and rife with bitterness, "but I am worried about the effect all of this is going to have on Pete."

Frank's mouth twisted in a derisive sneer. "Always the perfect mother, Caro. God, you've become a complete bore!"

"I admit our marriage hasn't been all it could have been, but at least I've never tried to ease my disappointment in someone else's bed."

"You wouldn't have had the guts."

Her shocked gasp drew his attention, and as the last remaining splotches of color drained from her cheeks, he hurriedly averted his eyes. "I'm sorry," he apologized in a more guarded tone. "I shouldn't have said that, but you have to admit you've always been a prude where sex is concerned, Caro."

In one sentence he had dealt a death blow to her pride in both her past purity and her present womanhood, and she was so hurt and angry that she felt as though the top of her head were going to burst. "I might have enjoyed sex more if you had ever been concerned with pleasing anyone but yourself."

He glared at her. "This isn't getting us anywhere."

Caroline agreed, and struggled against the urge to continue their verbal slanging match. Hang on, Caroline, she told herself staunchly as she lowered her head. Don't scream and cry or do any of the things you want to do, because you'll lose what little dignity you have left. She pulled a fuzzy ball free of her slacks, and stared at it in surprise.

When she began to roll it between her forefinger and thumb, the listlessness of her voice matched the movement of her hand. She returned to their original topic of discussion. "Pete isn't some casual acquaintance, Frank. He's our son, in case you've forgotten."

"For God's sake, the boy's nearly eighteen. He's not going to go into trauma because we're getting divorced."

He makes it sound as though we're joining the country club, she thought, the hurt a painful lump in her throat as she absorbed his sarcasm. But as always, he's right. I'm the only one in shock, and I don't matter to him any longer. His mistress is the one who's important to him now. The full realization of what was happening struck her, and she wanted to vomit.

Frank had just finished dumping a load of his sport shirts on the bed. The colorful garments lay beside his underwear, and her eyes lingered on his socks. They were carefully matched and folded the way Frank's fastidious nature demanded. She thought of all the hours and all the years she'd spent sorting and folding, and shuddered.

It was then they came, the words that bubbled up through her drying lips to ridicule her pride. They were pleading words, cajoling, and utterly humiliating. She heard herself reminding her stony-faced husband of the good times they'd shared, while she begged him to reconsider his decision. "How can you just throw away nearly twenty years of our lives as though they hold no value for you?" she asked in honest bewilderment.

"I'm through living on past memories, Caro."

His clipped statement eroded her self-control, and she began to voice the recriminations seething in her mind. The bedroom vibrated with the ugliness of vitriolic abuse, of thoughts that should have remained unspoken and of accusations that should have remained unthought. They tore at each other like two snarling animals, using petty spite as a destructive weapon until Caroline wished she could disappear. But it was Frank who was going away, and she stared across the room at the man who like a chameleon had slipped into the form of a hostile stranger.

Caroline wrapped her arms around her stomach and began rocking back and forth. "Oh, God! No more, no more...!"

Frank uttered an obscenity, his breathing audible. "Don't try laying a guilt trip on me, because it's not going to work. I never wanted to hurt you, Caro, but I can't help loving Priscilla. She makes me feel more alive than I've felt in years, and I refuse to go on day after day, bored out of my skull with discussions about clogged drains and whether or not we should have the furniture recovered."

"I never knew you felt that way," she protested, the words themselves an accusation. "Did you expect me to be a mind reader, Frank? Damn you! After all our years together, surely I deserved the courtesy of being given some kind of warning? We could have worked things out. We can still work together to save our marriage."

Frank shook his head, and Caroline experienced a sense of rejection greater than any she had ever known. She knew then the strength of the hold this other woman had on a man she had always considered to be hers, and could almost hear the fabric of her life being ripped apart.

"Don't look at me like that," Frank said. "I swear I didn't want to fall in love with Pris, it just happened. Can't you understand that?"

Oh, yes, she understood. Somewhere along the way Frank had become bored with his wife, and a bright new love had provided him with a means of escape. He would never take into consideration the fact that their relationship had fallen into a pattern that he himself had set. Too late, Caroline realized that she had allowed herself to be remade into what her husband had thought a wife should be. But now that the metamorphosis was complete, she thought bitterly, he was disenchanted with the result.

Frank had changed his priorities, and she had become too staid and predictable to hold him. Now the truth had to be faced, but she wasn't being given a hell of a lot of time to accomplish the feat. She was being dumped like so much unwanted garbage in favor of a nubile stranger. Frank no longer anticipated growing old with her...he expected to grow young with his Priscilla.

At this thought Caroline's chin went up, and her mouth firmed with righteous indignation. He claimed he had fought his attraction for this other woman, but she was through listening to anything he said. She just bet he had struggled nobly...all the way to the little bitch's bedroom. She said as much, and Frank's face mottled with a flush of rage.

He was voluble in defense of his ladylove, and during the unburdening process he was explicit in describing the perfections of his paramour. The words poured out of his mouth without a pause, as though he were trying to make up for never mentioning her before. What finally made Caroline angry was realizing the selfish idiot had waited until she'd fed him his dinner to do it.

"Are you going to marry her when the divorce is final?"

Now why in the world had she asked such a dumb question? When Frank left here tonight, his future happiness or misery would no longer be her concern. Then why was it that she only seemed to feel emptiness at the idea of someone else occupying her role in his life? she wondered. She felt as though a giant fissure had opened in her heart, draining away all emotion and leaving her incapable of feeling.

"That's none of your business."

Dear God, make the feeling come back, Caroline prayed with quiet desperation. She wanted... *needed*... to hate him. So while she tried to shut out the sound of his voice, Caroline kept her gaze riveted on his face. He was going on and on about alimony and child support, while snapping the locks on the bulging suitcase with a self-satisfied smirk.

Caroline saw him glance toward the clock to check the hour, and wondered if Miss Sexpot of the Year had given him a time limit. She could hear an imaginary voice in her mind, high-pitched and petulant. "I'll give you twenty minutes to tell your wife you're leaving her, darling, and another hour to pack. We're going to have such a lovely life together, Frankie, once you've managed to dump the old broad!"

Sweet heaven! Caroline thought. Was she slipping into the Twilight Zone, or simply trying to fashion herself after a potentially deranged Stephen King character? Her back was rigid with the need to shut Frank up, and she reached over to slam her hand against the clock radio's On button. The theme song from a popular nighttime talk show accompanied the movement of her steps as she rose to pace across the carpet.

The soles of her feet squished against the sticky nylon pile which Frank had picked up on sale, and she grimaced. She'd always hated nylon carpets, but as long as Frank had been pleased she hadn't complained. She speculated how happy he would have remained if he'd had to vacuum the damned thing. Come to think of it, she thought in belated defiance, she found the color nauseating.

Opposition to Frank's preference had always been something alien to her, conditioned as she had been to his dominance. Suddenly she found a little inward rebellion just what the doctor ordered. If she really wanted to indulge in some gut-level honesty, she thought, she would list all the reasons why their bedroom was her least favorite room in the entire house.

She suddenly wondered if Priscilla would ever lie staring resentfully at Frank's back, feeling alone and frustrated as she listened to him snore after they had sex.

A little laugh bubbled up in her throat, but was never given utterance. Since Frank's idea of making love consisted of accomplishing the act as hurriedly and functionally as possible, the phrase "had sex" was eminently suitable.

Frank grabbed his suitcase and began to move toward the door. "I'll be around in a few days to pick up the rest of my things," he said, tossing the words carelessly over his shoulder. "In the meantime, I'll have my lawyer call you."

Caroline resumed her position on the edge of the bed and studied her feet. The talk show host was ending his evening program, and she remembered other nights when his deep, sexy voice had sent shivers up her spine. But tonight the goose bumps covering her skin owed their existence to something quite different, she realized dully. Frank opened the door, and at the same moment a smoky drawl, rank with understated sensuality, requested his audience to have a good night. She watched her husband disappear down the hallway, his free and easy stride showing he hadn't a care in the world.

Caroline turned and glared at the radio. "Go suck eggs!"

The words were no sooner spoken when she heard Pete yelling at his father, then the sound of the front door slamming. Well, that cuts it, she thought. Frank was gone, and she was left sitting alone like an inanimate lump, inwardly vowing not to end up a piece of flotsam washed up on the shore of his life. She whispered a few of her son's choicest words and felt slightly better. She might have just become a damned statistic, but she was going to discover a bright side to all of this if it killed her.

"Mom, are you okay?"

Pete's large frame filled the doorway, and she turned to him with her version of a jaunty smile. Six feet tall in his stocking feet, with the midnight-black hair he'd inherited from her and his father's light blue eyes, he was quite a hunk, if she did say so herself. She supposed her opinion was slightly prejudiced, but it was shared by most of the female population of his high school. Yet at this moment it wasn't his good looks she appreciated, it was his obvious love and concern for her.

She beckoned him into the room, her voice cracking slightly as she said, "I'm fine, Pete."

"The no-good bastard!"

Pete snapped out his opinion with savage emphasis, and Caroline's grin slipped a little when she noted the anger and pity in his expression. The reassuring words she planned to speak died a quick death, but she did manage to hold onto the quirk at one side of her mouth. "That bastard's your father," she said almost choking, completely unaware of the ambiguity in her choice of phrase. "Show a little respect, Peter."

With a military salute he joined her on the bed, and his arm encircled her shoulders in an instinctive gesture of reassurance. "You've always insisted that I form my own opinions, Mother mine," he teased, squeezing her closer to his side. "You wouldn't want me to become a yes-man this late in the game, would you?"

Silence greeted his nervous quip, and he looked down at his mother's bent head. His hand tightened on her shoulder. "You'll be better off without him, Mom."

"Do you think so?" she responded dully.

"I'm going to see to it."

Glancing up at his scowling features, Caroline managed a shaky laugh. "What are you going to do, scalp him for me?"

"I might." He grinned.

Caroline tilted her head, a gleam of conjecture in her eyes. "I wonder if Priscilla knows his ears stick out when his hair's cut too short."

"Is that her name?"

Her eyes widened at the grimness of his expression. "You knew there was another woman?"

Pete set his jaw and avoided his mother's steady gaze. "Yeah, one of my friends saw them together."

"Why didn't you tell me?"

He shrugged with obvious embarrassment. "I was hoping the affair would burn itself out before you knew anything was going on," he admitted. "I wish now I'd warned you, but I didn't think Dad would be stupid enough to take things this far."

"He's in love." There was both sarcasm and anguish in her voice, and her shaking increased until her teeth began to chatter. "Oh, Pete, what do I do now?"

Pete embraced her and began to rock her in his arms. Caroline found a measure of comfort in the reversal of their roles and relaxed against him. "Let me lift his hair?" he asked, succeeding in making her smile.

Caroline lightly punched his chest with a curled fist. "As much as the thought appeals, it would be just my luck to have Precious Pris turned on by your father's shiny dome and flapping ears.''

Caroline twisted the ends of a towel just over her full breasts as she walked into her bedroom. She had taken as hot a shower as her sensitive skin would allow, but she wondered if she'd ever feel clean again. She still felt besmirched by the memory of the ugly scene that had occurred on this very spot mere hours ago. With a distracted air she brushed aside the curls clinging to her cheek.

She hadn't done a thorough job of blow-drying her hair, and a wild mass of dark curls framed her small features. The inky blackness against the pale oval of her face made her look like a Halloween witch, an impression undiminished by the steam that had fogged the bathroom mirrors. Feeling an unusual degree of nervousness she started toward her dresser to get her brush, but her feet faltered and then stopped entirely.

With a lackluster gaze she stared at the big bed dominating her surroundings. It looked as empty as she felt, and her lips pursed in distaste at the thought of climbing between the cold sheets. Quickly averting her head, she abruptly changed direction and walked toward the closet. But instead of reaching for her nightgown she paused with her hand in midair, an expression of shock on her face.

From the corner of her eye she saw the gaping hole where Frank's clothes had hung, and bit back a moan. Without being aware of making a decision she grabbed at a pair of emerald slacks, and automatically added the matching jewel-toned blouse hanging beside it. Her fingers trembled as she buttoned the blouse. Right now she needed as much color in her life as she could get.

After she was dressed, she rushed out of that place of unwelcome shadows, completely unconscious of using stealth as she tiptoed past Pete's room. Her only concern was to get out of a house filled with memories of a man who no longer lived there. She fumbled with the lock on the front door, feeling a sensation of almost desperate urgency.

Tonight the darkness held no terrors for her. She needed to fill the hours until dawn and didn't much care how she did it. All she could think of was walking until she was exhausted enough to sleep. But would she ever be able to sleep in that bed alone? she wondered with a shiver of revulsion. Would she even be able to return to that room without being haunted by Frank's cruel, emotionally destroying jibes at her femininity?

Caroline had forgotten to bring a coat, but the omission hardly registered in her dazed mind. She didn't feel the chill through her thin blouse, or the late-November breeze stinging her cheeks. When a light, drizzling mist began to fall from the darkening clouds overhead she quickened her pace, but never once thought of retracing her steps. For her, home had become just a word with no meaning or substance, filled with broken dreams and the memory of angry, unfor-givable words.

Pushing the unwelcome reminder aside she swal-lowed, nearly gagging on the dryness of her throat. Tilting back her head she opened her mouth to cap-ture the rain, which was now descending from the heavens in a torrent. Ahead of her the swift, angry flow of the American River beckoned, and for the first time she realized how far she'd wandered in her search for solace.

The moisture-whipped wind carried the scent of the river, and she suddenly longed to be closer to the storm-swollen waters. She didn't question her need. Some desperate part of her was reaching for the an-swers to a thousand questions, and she thought she might find what she was seeking if she got closer to one of the most natural forces on earth. Her eyes blinded by the lashing whip of the rain, she stepped into the street without noticing the dark shape plung-ing toward her.

Squealing brakes heralded its presence, and with instinctive haste Caroline leaped backward. The car's right front fender missed her by inches, and it was only the momentum of her body that knocked her to the ground. She lay on her back and tried to catch the breath that had been pushed from her lungs by the force of her fall, while her pulse pounded sickeningly in her ears.

Her eyelids felt so heavy that she closed them, too confused by the near accident to do more than lie quietly. Then the sound of running feet formed a counterpoint to her heartbeat, and a pair of strong hands pressed against her shoulders when she struggled to rise. "Are you all right?" a male voice inquired.

The brusque question with its underlying thread of anger didn't match the gentleness in the hands that held her, and her lashes sluggishly lifted in unwilling curiosity. She blinked to try and bring the face bending over her into focus, and blinked again when she partially succeeded. Although the streetlight behind him shrouded his features, she gained the impression of a broad forehead, thick, scowling brown eyebrows, a formidable nose, and a wide mouth tightly compressed into an angry slash. Eyes that seemed as fiery as the pits of hell glittered at her with banked rage in their depths, and a pair of wide shoulders cast an ominous shadow over her shivering body.

Caroline let her eyes close again and shook her head in confusion. The man resembled the Incredible Hulk, she decided, resisting a hysterical urge to giggle at the comparison. He seemed as big as a mountain, and if his expression was anything to go by, he was probably twice as hard. His voice had held a bit of a southern drawl, which didn't surprise her. She bet he was from Texas. Didn't they grow everything bigger in Texas? She gave a disgusted moan at the inanity of her mental ramblings, and stiffened when one of his hands began to travel over her left leg.

"Where do you hurt?"

This time the voice was slightly less brusque and held a gruff undertone of concern. Caroline tried to answer him, but her tongue seemed to have stuck itself to the roof of her mouth. As cold and wet as she was, she felt the warmth of his flesh scorch through her like summer lightning. Under the circumstances, the reaction of her body was ludicrous and demeaning. Although it had been months since Frank had touched her, that didn't explain why she should be overreacting to the physical presence of a stranger to this degree. If there was one thing she didn't need right now, she told herself sternly, it was a man. Especially one who looked as basically dominant and aggressively arrogant as this one did!

Two

___

His fingers squeezed her knee and shifted toward her thigh. Instinctively defensive, Caroline's hand jerked downward to impede their progress. The stern-visaged stranger muttered a terse imprecation, and her fingers were brushed aside with all the careless impartiality he would probably pay to a pesky fly. "I'm not trying to cop a feel," he growled impatiently, "so just lie still until I'm satisfied you haven't broken anything."

Her eyes popped open to glare up at him indignantly. "I'm going to have more bruises from being poked and prodded by you than from my fall."

He merely grunted, regarding her with piercing devil-dark eyes. "Did my car hit you?"

"No, I jumped back in time. I just had the breath knocked out of me."

Caroline averted her face from his contemplative gaze and tried to sit up. Instantly he shifted to restrain her, once more pressing her shoulders against the pavement. "Don't try to move," he demanded with an imperious self-assurance that made her see red, proving as it did that he hadn't listened to a word she'd said. "I have a phone in my car. It won't take me a minute to call for an ambulance."

Caroline was sick and tired of being advised and guided and bossed around by the male of the species, and there was both rebellion and resentment in her voice as she snapped, "I'm all right, or I would be if you'd just let me get up."

He hesitated a moment, then shifted his hands around to her upper back. Slowly he helped her into a sitting position, yet his large body remained poised over her hunched figure in a protective attitude. "Are you sure you're all right?"

The shock of the near accident had lifted the numbing fog from Caroline's mind and left her at the mercy of her emotions. Belated fright added an abruptness to her tone, making her sound coolly contemptuous when she muttered, "What do you want, a written affidavit? I told you I'm not hurt."

With his assistance she finally managed to get to her feet, only then becoming fully aware of how tall he was. He loomed over her own five feet four by at least a foot, and when his hands slid across her back to her arms, she gasped at the shiver of sensation that arched up her spine. With a jerky, stumbling gait she tried to pull away from him, irritated at being so intimidated by so much overpowering masculinity.

As though her defensive attitude set fire to dry tinder, the stranger's temper exploded. "Then you're damn lucky, lady. What in the hell were you trying to do, commit suicide?"

Caroline gasped at the ugliness of the accusation and struggled to free herself from the unyielding manacles his fingers had become. "Of course not!"

"You couldn't prove it by me. Of all the stupid, harebrained stunts to pull, this one tops the list. You need a keeper, do you know that? You're out wandering around alone in the middle of the night, easy prey for muggers or rapists or worse. Hell, you didn't even bother to put on a coat or a sweater to protect you from the rain. Then you go tripping off curbs without a thought for anyone but yourself, probably causing me to lose ten years of life in the process. Do you know what I thought when I saw you go down? Do you know what I felt when I thought I'd hit you? It's a wonder I didn't have a heart attack."

All Caroline could feel at the moment was his crushing grip against her shoulders as he shook her, and more of the numbness inside her was melted away by the heat of his anger. He had a right to be furious, but she was in no condition to offer him much of an explanation. With a low moan she tried to pull away from him, but only managed to lose her balance once again. It was the last straw, and with a tiny cry of defeat she slumped against his chest.

The arms wrapped around her now were less gentle than the hands had been, but she was grateful for their support as she swayed against the stranger's big body. Caroline had unwittingly used up her reserves of strength, and now her legs felt as weak as a newborn calf's. Why in hell shouldn't they? she asked herself in stunned comprehension. After what she'd been through tonight, it was a wonder she could stand at all.

Within the space of a few hours her husband had left her and she'd nearly been run down by a car. To top her entertaining evening, her soaking-wet body was plastered against a strange man's chest. And what a chest it was, she thought with an embarrassed quiver of realization. That muscled expanse could comfortably hold two women her size, and the man's height was formidable enough to block out the rest of the world with ease.

But Caroline's most disturbing realization came from within herself. She felt more than warm and safe in this man's embrace. Always honest with herself, she admitted that she was quite incredibly aroused. The sensations coursing through her were alien and confusing. She'd never reacted to any man like this in her life, not even to her husband in the early days of their courtship. This harsh-faced stranger seemed to possess a sensual current that leaped from his body to hers in an unbroken charge. The throb of her heartbeat had accelerated until she was choking on her own breath, and her tight, hard nipples were pressing against her bra as though seeking another resting place.

And Frank imagines I lead a dull life, she thought, her mouth forming a smile laced with bitterness. To her dismay she couldn't entirely stifle the giggle rising in her throat. Unfortunately her amusement was misconstrued, and the arms that tightened around her matched the rigidity of a tensely unyielding frame. "You find this situation amusing?"

Hearing the note of subdued anger in his gravelly voice, Caroline blinked nervously and tipped the raindrops from her lashes. Tilting her head back until his face came into view, she attempted to explain her odd behavior. "You don't understand. I . . ."

While their brief altercation had taken place, they had shifted positions. Now she was the one standing with her back to the streetlight, and found herself staring at one of the most handsomely forbidding faces she'd ever encountered. The illumination now filtering through the rain had become trapped in a pair of brown eyes, probably the most beautiful eyes she had ever seen. Their whiskey-colored surfaces were rimmed in gold, the subtle outline gaining depth in the darkness.

For all she knew, Caroline's enchanted scrutiny could have lasted for either seconds or minutes, because she lost all sense of time. With difficulty she finally tore her gaze away from those eyes, but only so that she could study the rest of her companion's features. She had already forgotten what she'd been intending to say to him, which was a good thing, since her throat didn't seem to be working properly, anyway. She felt the breath freeze in her lungs, and swallowed heavily.

Although he didn't appear to be more than four or five years older than her own thirty-seven, his dark brown hair was shot with luminous strands of silver gray. The cheekbones beneath his olive-tinted skin were prominent, his forehead broad, and his square chin sported a deep cleft in the middle. It was a forceful face, masculine and rugged, and yet there was a sensitivity in the curve of his mouth that belied the stern expression.

Even though his lips were tight with disapproval she noticed their fullness, hinting at a sensuality she was loath to acknowledge. Yet she didn't have much choice. Now she couldn't seem to be able to tear her gaze away from that mouth, no matter how hard she tried, and a shudder of awareness rippled through her. She could feel the warmth of his flesh against her breasts, as though the clinging fabric between them didn't exist. She wished it didn't, and that thought shocked her into another fiercer, betraying shiver.

Caroline saw his lips move, but couldn't hear a word he said over the sudden roar of thunder overhead. A wild gust of wind whipped her soaking hair across her cheek, and she absentmindedly brushed aside the clinging strands. "What?" she asked in dazed confusion.

He bent closer, and his breath seemed to scorch heat across her ear. "I said the storm's getting worse, and you've got to get out of this downpour. You must be freezing without a coat."

Even while he spoke he was shrugging out of the trench coat he was wearing over a dark blue suit. He draped the garment over her shoulders with a gentlemanly flourish, but she was too busy bristling at the disapproval in his voice to appreciate the courtesy. "It wasn't raining when I left."

The outer tip of one dark, slashing eyebrow quirked at her belligerence, but he didn't respond verbally. Instead he slipped an arm around her waist and began leading her toward his car. When he held the passenger door open for her she halted and gave him a doubtful glance. "I don't think—"

"No, it doesn't appear as though you do much thinking," he interrupted sarcastically. "You may like standing here in danger of drowning, but I sure as hell don't. Now you can either get in my car before you catch your death or I'll put you in. The choice is yours."

"Then I choose to leave the same way as I arrived!"

Pivoting on her heel, Caroline was mentally congratulating herself on her inner fortitude when she was pulled up short by an unrelenting grip on her forearm. Looking down at his circling fingers with disdainful emphasis, she muttered, "You can cut the Sir Galahad routine and let me go. You may think I'm some kind of flaky female without the sense God gave a mouse, but I can assure you that I'm too smart to get in that car with you. I'm fully capable of getting home on my own two legs, thank you very much.''

"You might not care about your own safety, but I'd like to be able to sleep tonight. Which is something I won't do if I'm worrying about some dumb broad without the sense God gave a flea, let alone a mouse. You really do need a keeper, lady.''

"I had one of those, but he walked out on me tonight.''

Appalled by the admission, Caroline clamped her fingers over her mouth and felt the metallic smoothness of her wedding band against her lips. Slowly she lowered her hand. Her eyes were huge as she stared at the golden circle that was supposed to mean a beginning without end. Forever, she thought as her chest tightened with agonizing emotion. Now the ring represented nothing, she thought dully. Nothing....

Caroline's movements were suddenly frantic as she pulled and twisted the ring from her finger. Then it was there, lying in her palm, and as she stared at it she loathed everything it represented. Hopes and dreams that were as dead as the love it had once symbolized, memories that had sweetened her past and now soured her future; the young girl who, somewhere along the road of wedded bliss, had somehow lost the woman she might have become. With a strangled cry she clenched her fist, drew back her arm, and threw the cold, glittering piece of jewelry into the darkness where it belonged. Her chest heaved with the effort it took not to cry.

After a moment she lifted her head and saw a flash of compassion in his eyes. She could deal with mockery, scorn, sarcasm, or even outright hostility, but compassion was beyond her ability to bear. Without warning she began to cry, not daintily with controlled, ladylike decorum but harshly, wrenchingly, until her entire body was shaking with hysterical sobs.

A voice whispered in her ear, its tones heavy with remorse. "Oh, God, I'm sorry."

The admission was bitten off as he suddenly bent and lifted her into his arms, his features hard and expressionless as he tenderly lowered her into his car. Caroline moaned, her hands covering her face as she tried to regain her composure. "I'm the one wh-who's s-sorry."

But all the pain and grief and anguished emotions held her in thrall, and she couldn't seem to stop the flow of tears. They'd been damned up inside her for too long. She hadn't let herself cry tonight in front of Frank, and the determination that had formed a barrier to their release had finally deserted her. When the stranger opened the driver's door and joined her on the plush seat of his luxurious Cadillac, pride no longer seemed so important to Caroline. Only the reassuring feel of being held and comforted had any meaning.

"Go ahead and cry," he whispered against the top of her head as he drew her close. "Get it all out of your system, honey. I know what this kind of pain is like, so don't be embarrassed. No one deals well with rejection from someone they once trusted enough to love, but the hurt eases in time."

Caroline lowered her hands to her lap and gazed blankly at the mark where her ring used to be, while the evidence of her rage and grief trickled against the corners of her trembling mouth. She licked at the betraying moisture, her voice barely audible as she said, "He... he just left, with no warning. I've known for months that something was bothering him. It was fairly obvious, when even a perfunctory goodbye kiss in the morning became more of an effort than he wanted to expend on me. But since Frank's never been overly demonstrative, I just put it down to midlife crisis or something. I don't know why I never suspected that there might be a... another woman."

The shake of her head expressed both despondency and anger. "I was so stupid," she muttered. "So blind and idiotically naive!"

"You trusted him," he remarked softly. "That's nothing to reproach yourself for."

Caroline sent a scathing glance in his direction. "Look where all my trust got me. She has my husband and I have nothing."

A muscle pulsed in his jaw as he clamped his teeth together, and a strange expression glittered briefly in his eyes. He started to speak, but seemed to change his mind with an abruptness that startled her. Tearing his gaze away from her face, he turned his key in the ignition.

"Where are you taking me?" she cried in a shaking voice.

"Where do you want to go?"

"I don't want to go home," she gasped. "Please don't take me home."

"I won't," he promised hurriedly, looking at her with a worried frown. "But you've got to get out of those wet clothes or you'll end up sick."

Caroline shook convulsively, her expression haunted. "I can't go back, not yet."

He twisted the steering wheel, briefly checking for any traffic before he accelerated into the street. "Look, my place is just around the corner. Will you go there with me?"

Her sobs had eased into a few raspy hiccups, and she sniffled like a child as she nodded in agreement. "My name's Caroline."

He grinned as he pulled up to a stop sign and turned to shake hands with mocking formality. "Mine is James."

Heat seemed to radiate from their palms, and their glances locked together in a quiet moment of discovery. Releasing her hand, James lifted one finger to trace the trembling outline of her mouth. Caroline tensed at the gentle touch, but didn't pull away. She felt no sense of threat from this man, only a kindness that caught at her heart. A slow warmth was replacing the coldness inside her, a warmth caused by the intensity of his gaze as he studied her emotion-ravaged features.

Self-consciously Caroline stared at the cleft in his chin. "Don't look at me. I'm a mess."

"You're beautiful."

Her head jerked up at the quiet sincerity in his voice, which seemed to lend emphasis to his statement. "Should a man in your condition be driving this thing?"

"A man in my condition?"

Caroline nodded with solemn brevity. "Half-blind."

The corner of his mouth twitched and a low, raspy chuckle emerged from his throat. "You have a be-witching sense of honesty about you, but for your in-formation my vision's twenty-twenty. Your face is a delicately shaped oval, your green eyes are like morn-ing sunlight on a leaf, and your mouth holds a gentle curve. Any man would think you as lovely as a dream, Caroline."

"Except my husband," she replied despondently. "For him I've become a nightmare."

He snorted derisively. "The man's a fool."

Caroline was cheered by his comment and re-sponded with a shy smile. "Thank you, James."

Golden eyes glittered briefly at the sound of his name on her lips, and his movements were tense and oddly uncoordinated as he returned his attention to the road. Completely unaware that his reaction was in any way unusual, Caroline leaned her head back against

the soft upholstery with a sigh. As the car moved
through the darkness, she felt strangely content.

Caroline didn't see that her rescuer glanced repeatedly at her profile, nor that bold male awareness shone
in his eyes. The mouth she'd so recently admired softened with sensuality, and over the sound of the rain he
murmured, "His loss is my gain, sweet Caroline."

James ushered Caroline through his front door with
a distinct feeling of anxiety. He wanted her to like his
home, which he'd had built and decorated to suit his
individual style. He didn't want to think about why it
mattered so much to him that she feel comfortable in
a place uniquely his own, and his cowardly self-
evasion brought a rueful quirk to his lips.

Sweet heaven, he thought disbelievingly, he hadn't
reacted to a woman like this in years. For just a moment his eyes held shadows of the past, his mind hesitating with almost physical reluctance at the memory
of another woman. She had been tall and blond and
quite strikingly beautiful, and he had been too enam-
ored to see through the outer package to the coldness
of her soul.

He had married her and been trapped in the frozen
wasteland of his own emotions. With queenly ele-
gance she had given him her presence in his life, as
though bestowing a great gift on an undeserving subject. But that was all she had given, just the outline
with no substance. There had been no passion for him,
only for the career she was determined to succeed in,

no matter what the cost. Well, she had succeeded, he thought bitterly, thanks to the assistance he had given her. Then she had turned her back and gotten on with the job, marking him as finished business and leaving him behind.

With quiet fascination he watched as Caroline stepped past the hardwood-floored entry and into the sunken living room. His gaze was intent as he studied her bedraggled figure, and he found himself wondering just what it was about her that he found so appealing. Her wet hair had formed springy little curls that framed her face like a silky black halo, her widely spaced, thickly lashed green eyes still had a spark of determination, and there was a tired, dispirited curve to her small, exquisitely shaped mouth.

Not a face to set the world on fire . . . only him. He wanted to kiss the sadness from those pouting lips and wipe away the pain from those lovely eyes. He wanted to strip the wet clothing from her body and warm her with his heat. He wanted, he admitted ruefully, altogether too much from a woman he hadn't even known two hours ago. But when he tried to analyze his reaction to her, he failed to reach any kind of logical conclusion. He didn't understand why her appeal was so great, or why his need was so strong. He only knew that he craved her gentleness like a man dying of thirst in the desert, and he sensed an underlying need in her that matched his own.

Caroline's footsteps were tentative, her manner uncertain as she glanced at the high peaked roof and

beamed ceilings overhead. The contemporary furnishings formed a striking contrast to the wooden accents throughout the open living area. The walls were
white, but except for the raised entry dais the front
wall was almost entirely of glass from the pale green
carpeted floor to the cathedral ceiling. To her left a
modular sofa unit was set in a semicircle to gain full
advantage of the view from the windows, and its clean,
elegant lines were covered in a cream material with a
leaf pattern. Coffee and end tables were glass-topped
with curved, lustrous brass bases.

"This room is lovely," Caroline whispered in awe-
struck tones. She looked at the large basket-potted
trees in the corners, the hanging ferns that were reflected in the slightly smoked glass of the windows,
and the sparse but beautiful furnishings. When she
turned to face him, there was an expression of delight
on her face. "I feel as though I've stepped into a for-
est glade."

The room was bathed in light from the fixtures set
into the dark beams overhead, and for the first time
James was able to distinguish the exact color of her
eyes. His breath caught in his throat. They were paler
than he'd realized, and outlined by darker rings. The
eyes of Circe, he thought, mysterious and compel-
ling. He stared in fascination as they seemed to absorb both light and shadow, and a sensation very close
to pain lanced his body.

When Caroline looked at him he wanted to wipe
away the shadows that obviously lingered in the depths

of those eyes, leaving behind only the light to warm his soul. He had been cold and lonely for so long that he'd become accustomed to the emptiness that governed his life, he realized, and this sudden thaw of his emotions had an unbearable poignancy. He felt a surge of protectiveness and a powerful, gut-wrenching need to possess. Finally he understood why human beings had persisted for so long while other life-forms had become extinct.

Caroline turned to study the room further, and James suddenly discovered he was having a great deal of difficulty breathing. She looked so vulnerable and defenseless, and so damned alone. His hands clenched into fists at his sides. No woman as gentle and lovely as Caroline should be unloved, he thought achingly. With a swift surge of triumph he also knew that this was the one woman who could put an end to his own loneliness.

Three

James's thoughts reformed when he saw Caroline shiver convulsively. Quickly he stepped forward and grasped her elbow to guide her down a wide hallway to his right, the rain bulleting against a long skylight set in the ceiling. "You've got to get into a hot bath," he said, his voice as quiet and calming as he could make it, considering the extent of his emotional reaction to her. "I'm going to take a shower upstairs and get into dry clothes, so don't hurry on my account. Have a good long soak to chase the chill from your bones."

He glanced down at her feet and grinned. "Speaking of bones, I'm afraid my slippers wouldn't stay on those tiny feet of yours. Would you like to use a pair of my socks?''

Caroline avoided his eyes and shook her head, chattering to alleviate her uneasiness. "Don't worry, I'll be all right barefoot. Your carpeting is so thick and soft, my feet will think I've died and gone to heaven. This deep pile looks as warm as toast, a far cry from the sticky nylon monstrosity I've got at home.''

She had to bite her lip to keep herself from any further blathering. A slight flush of embarrassment added a hint of color to her pale cheeks as she glared down at the floor. She was a true sophisticate, all right, she decided in disgust. Here she was alone with a virile, handsome man and she was getting into an in-depth discussion on carpets! It didn't take much effort for her to imagine the derisive sneer on Frank's face if he could see her now.

James hid a smile behind his hand, coughing to hide the laugh that was threatening to betray his amusement. This woman was as skittish as a filly being broken to halter, and he didn't have to ask to know she was out of her depth in this kind of situation. He'd never met any female less likely to allow herself to be picked up and taken home by a man, much less by a man who was a total stranger. He was surprised by how pleased he was at the realization, and his voice was a low, soothing drawl laced with understanding as he said, "I want you to be comfortable, Caroline."

"Thank you, you're very kind."

The timid reply was barely audible. Now Caroline
was intently studying the wide double doors they'd
stopped in front of, as though fascinated by the deep
whorls hand-carved into the surface of the wood. She
was doing her level best to avoid looking at him, and
he took full advantage of the opportunity it afforded
him. Tenderly he glanced down at her bent head.

He drew in a swift breath as a jolt of desire flooded
through him. He wanted to tangle his fingers in her
midnight-black curls and absorb the dampness from
each strand with his palms. He wanted to press his
mouth against that fluttery little pulse he saw beating
against her throat, and warm her cold flesh with the
warmth from his body.

With a great deal of difficulty he put a damper on
his thoughts, and threw open the door of the guest
room to lead her inside. He was blind to the lustrous
beauty of the cherry-wood furniture and the rose and
cream damask curtains framing the bow-fronted window embrasure, his mind preoccupied with defusing
some of the tension between Caroline and himself.

With attempted casualness James gestured toward
a far door. "There's a third bathroom at the end of the
hall, but I think you'll enjoy the Jacuzzi in this one.
The On switch and heat regulator are set in the wall
panel opposite the taps. One of my robes is hanging on
the back of the bathroom door, there's a hair dryer
under the center cabinet, and fresh towels are on the
rack. I think you'll find everything you need," he re-

marked with formal courtesy. "If not, just give me a yell."

Her head jerked up, her gaze wide and nervous as she studied his suddenly distant features. "Where... where shall I go after I'm through?"

"I'll make some hot coffee and have it waiting for you in the living room." James's smile felt wooden, his body tight and stiff as he turned away from a temptation that was growing stronger with every second that passed.

"James?"

He froze with his back to her, wanting to hear her ask him to stay. A beguiling vision of his hands reaching out to help Caroline remove her sodden clothing shimmered before his inner eye. Just the thought of sharing her bath was enough to make him shudder with longing. He ached to make the suggestion himself but could just imagine how she'd react. Clearing his throat of the forbidden words, he finally managed a clipped response. "Yes?"

"Thank you again," she whispered on a quavering note.

Caroline watched him leave with mixed feelings churning in her breast. Feeling the discordant beat of her heart through every inch of her body, in a gesture of nervousness she pressed one hand against her chest. She wandered into the bathroom and glanced around in confusion. She was experiencing a strange sense of disassociation, as though the image staring at her from the mirror fitted against the cream-colored wall was a woman she'd never seen before.

She had been tested by fire and had reemerged half-formed, she thought whimsically. Her impression of herself had altered in some basic, fundamental way. She was neither married nor single, yet she was both free and a prisoner of her own nature. A sudden memory rose to haunt her, the sarcastically chiding voice reverberating in her mind. *You wouldn't have the guts!*

Frank thought her too staid and old and predictable to have an affair, and he was right. She couldn't imagine herself being intimate with a man other than her husband, and even with him she'd never been any great shakes in the sensuality department. "Couldn't you imagine it with a man as attractive and considerate as James?" a slyly tempting inner voice taunted. "He wouldn't be a selfish lover concerned only with his own satisfaction." Shocked at the sudden trembling rippling through her body, she shook her head in a wild gesture of repudiation. Was she losing her mind? she asked herself disgustedly, as she clumsily began to strip herself of her wet clothing.

If not relaxed, Caroline at least felt warmer after taking a hot bath. The large sunken tub had been an experience in luxury, but she hadn't been at ease with such opulence. She was a bread-and-butter kind of woman, she decided wryly, which was one of the reasons she was here. She wondered if James preferred bread and butter, or if, like Frank, he had a hunger for croissants and honey.

While rubbing herself dry with one of the large, fluffy towels she had pulled from a heated rack, she contemplated the unexpected course her life had taken. Soon she would be Frank's ex-wife, and from the way he'd extolled the virtues of his mistress, she suspected it wouldn't be long before that other woman would have the right to call herself Mrs. Barclay. The realization was bewildering as well as painful. She cringed from the finality of the decision her husband had made such a short time ago, while in the same instant becoming aware that his switch in allegiance had caused her to question her own identity in a way she hadn't done in years.

Just who is Caroline Barclay? she asked herself silently. Is she the shy, introverted high-school student who thought the sun rose and set in the blue eyes of the college boy next door? Is she the eighteen-year-old girl who left her parents to begin life with a man she was sure would love her forever? Is she the young matron who foolishly subjugated her preferences in favor of her husband's? Or is she the woman with the bitter, disillusioned eyes she just glimpsed in the mirrored glass?

With a gasp Caroline whirled and reached for the burgundy robe hanging on the back of the door. The thick, soft velour was soft against her palms, but the thing was huge. She suspected it must fit James about midknee, but she would be lucky if she didn't trip over the hem and break both of her legs. Still, she decided bracingly, if she wrapped it around herself and tightened the belt, she would be decently covered.

At least it was a man's garment, she thought, surprised to realize she wouldn't have found it nearly as acceptable to wear if it had been fashioned for a woman. A man like James would have women, probably a lot of women. He was too sensual a man to live like a monk, and she was suddenly curious about his preferences in females. Did he favor blondes, or redheads? Did he like them tall or short, petite of full-figured, or did he . . . ? It's none of your business, she interrupted herself angrily, snorting in disbelief at the fantasies she was weaving in her too-fertile imagination.

Caroline momentarily crushed the soft fabric of the robe between betrayingly unsteady hands, before slipping her arms through the sleeves and cuffing them until her fingers were uncovered. After the tie belt was snugly in place she glanced down at the hem, which brushed against her rounded calves. Well, she wouldn't be tripping over the thing after all, she thought, a rueful grin curving her lips as she remembered her earlier exaggerated certainty. It was odd how, whenever she was uncomfortable with a given situation, her mind envisioned all the many ways she could make a fool of herself. She wondered if self-consciousness was determined by genetics.

On that thought Caroline gathered up her clothes and tiptoed from the bathroom. She hurried across the bedroom with its sensuously warm decor, and breathed a sigh of relief when she emerged into the hallway. Hesitating with characteristic timidity, she felt like some kind of Little Orphan Annie as she stood poised beneath the arched entry to the living room.

James had started a fire, and stood with one arm resting against the carved wooden mantel as he studied the flickering flames. Although she ached to move into the warmth, she felt paralyzed with shyness. In desperation she cleared her throat, knowing if she didn't catch his attention immediately she was most likely to turn tail and run. She fought down a mortifying urge to laugh and clamped her lips tightly together. When it came right down to it, she thought in disgust, cowardice was probably a genetic fault, too.

James started with surprise and raised his head. The instant his eyes met Caroline's, the distance separating them became negligible. His gaze slid from the top of her curly head to the tips of her bare toes in a thoroughly masculine appraisal, and she felt as though an unseen force was pulling her forward. "I . . . uh, here are m-my clothes," she stammered self-consciously.

With a smile of approval, he strolled forward with a confident manner she envied. As he took the clothing from her, he waved his other hand toward the glass-topped coffee table. "Pour yourself a cup of coffee while I put these in the dryer."

She nodded, and he promised huskily, "I won't be a minute."

The low tones caused a shiver to race down her spine, and she watched him walk away with bated breath. He moved with sinuous grace for such a large man, and she found herself unable to tear her gaze from his tall frame until he disappeared from sight. What's happening to me? she wondered in a half-terrified daze. Since she'd first set eyes on James, her body had seemed to be composed of nothing but nerve ends and rampant hormones. The knowledge was frightening. She'd never reacted to a man so...so physically before! Even in the early days of her relationship with Frank she'd never experienced this maelstrom of emotions.

"There, that didn't take long."

When James's voice sounded so close beside her, Caroline jumped about a foot in the air and uttered a strangled cry. She whirled with a panic-stricken expression on her face, and he was instantly contrite. "Caroline, just relax and drink your coffee," he urged gently. "I'm not going to jump on you the minute you lower your guard."

Her cheeks bloomed with color once more, and she moved stiffly when he waved her toward the sofa. She was relieved to be able to sit down, because she doubted if her shaking legs were going to hold her up much longer. Dancing flames were trapped within the smooth silver of the coffee urn in front of her, as was her disturbed reflection. She grimaced self-consciously, glancing at him tentatively from beneath half-lowered lids. "I'm sorry I'm not more sophisticated."

"Don't apologize for being yourself, honey. I know you feel uncomfortable alone here with me, but you've got nothing to worry about. To be completely honest, I'm a little uneasy in this situation myself. You're not the kind of woman I'm used to entertaining, and you make me nervous."

Her eyes widened. "I make you nervous?"

James laughed at the incredulity in her voice, and nodded. "Does that surprise you?"

"Astounds is more like it," she admitted, her expression frankly curious as she looked at him. "I'm so plain and ordinary. Why should I make you nervous?"

"Because to me you're unique and far from plain. I know this sounds rather lame, but you have such beautiful, kind eyes, Caroline."

She flushed at the compliment and said softly, "It doesn't sound at all lame."

With quick, economical movements he poured the steaming dark liquid into a cup and handed it to her. "Do you take cream and sugar?"

The prosaic question made her smile, and the revelation that he was doing his best to alleviate her fears added a radiance to her face that James noticed, but of which she was unaware. "Just a little cream, please."

After pouring himself a cup of the fragrant brew he reclined on the cushion next to her with a sigh of appreciation. He had changed into a blue pullover sweater and a pair of brushed denims. After giving him a quick glance from the corner of her eyes, Caroline kept her attention focused on her coffee. She was more aware of the snug fit of those jeans and the way that soft-looking sweater clung lovingly to the muscled hardness of his chest than she wanted to admit.

James shifted his broad shoulders against the back of the sofa and levered a bare foot beneath his thigh as he turned toward her. "Feel a bit warmer?"

Warm wasn't the word for what she was feeling, but Caroline decided that now wasn't the time to get into a technical discussion on body temperature. "I'm fine, thank you," she murmured with a primness she deplored.

Lazily he shook his head, an amused quirk to his mouth as he looked at her. His voice was teasing as he asked, "Are you always this polite, Caroline?"

Her hand trembled slightly as she raised the cup to suddenly parched lips. After taking a reviving sip of coffee she shrugged and tonelessly remarked, "My husband has another name for it. He thinks I'm rather a dull stick."

"Then he's a moron," James retorted without hesitation.

Caroline's entire body quivered, and in an effort to hide her reaction she drained the contents of her cup in one gulp. The inside of her mouth felt as hot as the rest of her, but she tamped down her embarrassment enough to respond. "He's not really a moron, just a man looking for the gold at the end of the rainbow. No better or worse than any other man," she concluded bitterly.

"Any man with half a brain wouldn't discard gold in favor of dross."

Caroline's breath caught on a sigh, and there was a hint of moisture glistening in the depths of her eyes as she whispered, "You don't know how much I needed to hear that, James. I'm so angry and filled with resentment, and I don't like feeling that way. I've spent years being the wife I thought Frank wanted, but somewhere alone the line he changed his priorities without letting me know.

"I've cooked his meals on time, kept his home clean, and entertained his clients. I've run a thousand and one errands for him, washed his clothes, and starched and ironed his shirts because he preferred cotton to permanent press. I've tried to be the best wife possible for him, and tonight he told me how deadly dull I've become. I modeled my entire life to suit his needs, and now I'm just a boring irritation to be gotten rid of as quickly as possible."

"You're not boring," James blurted, his features grim as he absorbed her pain. "You're a bit on the shy side, but you're also sweet and gentle and lovely. My first impression of your husband was the correct one. If he's too blind to see what he's throwing away, then the man's a moron. And if this is the way he rewards his wife's loyalty, then he doesn't deserve you."

A tiny grin teased the corner of her mouth. "That's pretty much what my son Peter said, only he used a stronger descriptive word. In his younger years I would have washed his mouth out with soap."

James stiffened, jealousy toward the man he'd just derided tightening his insides. "You have children?"

"Just Pete." She wrinkled her nose at him and laughed. "By the way, if you know what's good for you, you'll never refer to a seventeen-year-old male as a child within his hearing."

James studied his finger, which was tracing the pattern of a leaf on the sofa arm. "I wouldn't know, since I've never had the opportunity to learn much about children. My ex-wife was obsessed with her career and didn't want any. It was a sore point between us, but after she walked out on me I was glad there weren't any kids to suffer for our mistakes."

"Now I understand why you're so sympathetic toward me," she whispered softly.

He lifted his head, his gaze trapped by the sympathy in her eyes. "I beg your pardon?"

"You said she walked out on you, so you know how it feels to be discarded."

He nodded, his jaw hardening. "We were both used in different ways, Caroline. You for convenience, and me as a step up on my ex's ladder to success. It leaves a nasty taste in the mouth and murder in the heart, but the pain and anger do pass eventually."

"It's getting to 'eventually' that I'm worried about," she admitted wryly. "A change in life-style might be best for me in the long run, but I don't even know where to start. And then there's Pete. He's in his senior year of high school, and I'm worried about how all this is going to affect him. I don't want the normal pattern of his life disturbed any more than it has to be, but we may have to sell the house and move to a more affordable location. Support from Frank won't be enough to maintain our household expenses, and thanks to his 'a woman belongs in the home' philosophy, I've never had a job. The only work I've ever done has been in a volunteer capacity, and I don't think that's going to be much of an incentive for any prospective employer to hire me.''

James's first reaction was to offer her a job, but the words froze in his throat. The past rose up to haunt him as he remembered how he had given his ex-wife the job she coveted and become a means to an end. He hadn't enjoyed being used. As a result, in all his relationships since his divorce he'd been careful to choose women already well established in their own careers. The females in his employ had been kept strictly off limits, and he wanted to keep it that way.

For as long as he could remember, he had found it difficult to trust women. His own mother had been a cool, formally correct individual who disdained emotionalism. His father had been the one to provide the affection he'd craved, but had been killed in a boating accident just before James's tenth birthday. He supposed his mother had done the best she could under the circumstances, but it hadn't been enough. He'd spent most of his formative years living in private schools, and his visits with his mother had been stilted and uncomfortable occasions. Only her sense of duty and obligation had prompted them, and until the day she died they'd remained strangers to each other.

But listening to Caroline talk about marriage had given him an entirely different perspective on his own life. He'd never had anyone to care about his comfort and happiness the way she had cared about her husband's, and the jealousy he felt toward the other man increased until he was startled by its intensity. God, what he wouldn't give to be loved like that! She might be insecure and frightened, but he sensed a strength in Caroline that would cause her to triumph over adversity. That strength lay in her ability to love selflessly. It was a rare quality, and he was certain that her concern for her son would give her the impetus she needed to overcome any future difficulties she might face.

He told her as much, adding, "Pete's a damn lucky kid to have you."

"He's never been as close to his father as I would have liked. Frank's always been too involved in wheeling and dealing real estate to have much time for his son, and Pete quite naturally resented it. I'm afraid Frank did, too, but he always blamed me for alienating Pete's affection."

"It's a lot easier to blame someone else for our own shortcomings."

Her mouth twisted cynically. "After the things Frank said to me tonight, he made me all too aware of mine."

"Don't let him ease his conscience by placing all the blame onto you," he retorted angrily. "It takes two to make a marriage, and two to break it."

"But he was right," she whispered, her eyes filled with shadows of memory. "I wrapped myself up in my safe little cocoon of domesticity, and failed to see that my husband needed someone who could understand the pressures and problems he faced outside the home."

"Bull!"

Caroline stiffened and glared at him. "What do you mean?"

"I said bull and I meant it." He ran his hand over his hair in an exasperated gesture and glared back at her. "If I'm getting a clear picture of your marriage, your precious Frank had everything just the way he wanted it. He had you to keep him comfortable, and a career to satisfy his ambition. If he'd wanted to share those career aspirations with you he would have, and you know damn good and well that you wouldn't have had to sell real estate yourself to understand his problems."

She trembled at the force of his anger, but it wasn't fear of James that caused her to shake. She was gaining a new perspective on herself, one so different from her husband's that she was almost afraid to believe in it. Tentatively she whispered, "Frank said it drove him crazy talking about clogged drains and—"

"Then he should have shared himself with you and given you something else to talk about."

She winced at the forcefulness of his assertion and glanced away from him. She hesitated, her voice a mere thread of sound as she admitted, "I failed him in...other ways."

"I'd like to know how!"

James was breathing heavily as he tried to regain a little control over his seething emotions. He was beginning to realize why Caroline lacked confidence in herself, and didn't like the conclusions he'd reached. He saw a gentle woman vulnerable to criticism, and a selfish man adept at preying on that vulnerability to gain his own ends. The thought of Caroline being a victim of that kind of mind game enraged him, and his voice was sharper than he intended when he snapped, "What in the hell more could a man expect from his wife?"

"A little more eagerness in bed!"

Caroline had responded to his aggressive attitude instinctively, before she'd had time to think. As soon as she heard the words tripping so bitingly off her wayward tongue, she wanted to fall through the floor. She was horrified at having exposed her most intimate secrets to a man who was, when it came right down to it, a total stranger.

"I'm sorry," she murmured. "I'm sorry for burdening you with my troubles. I...think it's time I went home."

James noted her embarrassed confusion, but decided to deal with it in as prosaic a manner as possible. Reaching forward, he relieved her of the empty cup and set it beside his on the coffee table. Then he draped his arm across the back of the sofa and leaned forward until she was compelled to look at him. "Why?"

"B-because my clothes will be dry, and I—"

"Why aren't you eager in bed, Caroline?"

She swallowed uncomfortably, enthralled by the way his eyes suddenly glowed with a golden light. "I...I guess I'm frigid."

He barely heard the whispered admission before he was shaking his head, his expression holding the certainty of a man confident of the rightness of his own opinions. "He's really done a job on you, hasn't he?"

"I don't know what you mean."

"I mean that you're about as frigid as I am," he murmured gently. "And I can assure you that I'm not."

This time Caroline's throat was so corded with tension that she couldn't even swallow. Sometime during the last few minutes James had drawn even closer to her, and she felt overpowered by the sheer masculine aura he projected. In an attempt to give herself a little breathing space she tilted back her head, and felt it land against his hard biceps. She gasped at the contact, and questioned shakily, "You're not?"

James found that little squeak in her voice enchanting, but even more endearing was the way her soft lips trembled when she gazed at his mouth. "I'm not."

At that point Caroline didn't know quite where to look, so she lowered her eyes to his chest. That proved to be a mistake, because the sight of golden-brown hair escaping from the V neckline of his sweater increased her heartbeat to an alarming degree. Deciding conversation might help to lower her blood pressure, she began to chatter. "Frank just doesn't find me as attractive as his mistress, and I can't really blame him. I'm not the kind of woman a man loses his head over."

She plastered what she hoped passed as a carefree smile onto her lips, and once again found the courage to search his bold features. She heard him draw in his breath, while her own breathing stopped entirely. Their eyes met in a glance so heated that she felt her toes curl. An almost visible tension was lanced between them when he probed her bottom lip with a caressing thumb. "That depends on the man, Caroline."

Four

Caroline desperately wanted to believe the message she saw in his eyes, but was too certain of her own shortcomings as a woman to be taken in by his compassion. James was basing his opinion of her on a first impression, but Frank had lived through years of marriage with her. James was only trying to make her feel better, but she didn't want lies to make her situation more palatable. If she was the kind of woman he was describing, then why was another woman sleeping with her husband at this very moment?

Unexpected pain ripped through her until she wanted to scream, and she closed her eyes against it. "Stop being so kind, damn it! If there's one thing I don't need or want, it's your pity."

His response was dry and to the point. "You're more naive than I thought, if you think all I'm feeling right now is pity."

"What else can it be?"

James slid his thumb from her mouth to her cheek, picking up a single teardrop along the way. "I want you," he remarked bluntly. "Is that straightforward enough for you?"

She flinched and reluctantly opened her eyes. "I don't need to be pacified as though I were a sulking child."

His voice flat and toneless, he stated, "You don't believe me."

Caroline shrugged, feigning unconcern. "Let's just say that I have a great many reservations and leave it at that."

He shook his head, his gaze intent as he studied her evasive mannerisms. "I'm not willing to ignore or evade what's happening between us, nor am I willing to excuse it as basic chemistry, Caroline."

"Isn't that all it is?" she argued, giving him a pointed glance before she quickly looked at a distant point over his shoulder. "The way we met was rather dramatic, you have to admit."

"What does that have to do with anything?"

"Quite a lot, if you'd just stop to think about it," she remarked impatiently. "It's been obvious from the first that you're a kindhearted man, James. Almost running me over brought all your protective instincts to the surface, and listening to my troubles has only honed those instincts. This entire situation isn't real for either of us, can't you see that?''

He lowered his hand until his thumb and forefinger could pinch the edge of her rounded chin. With a gentle pressure he tilted her head until she was forced to look at him, his eyes darkening with brooding intensity as he gazed into hers. ''Fate threw us together at a time when we were both vulnerable, darlin'. The timing may be off, but that doesn't lessen the impact of what's happened.''

''Nothing's happened,'' she muttered with stubborn insistence. ''It's late, we're a man and a woman alone by a warm fire, and I, for one, am under a considerable amount of emotional stress. You're feeling normal urges and I happen to be handy.''

''I'm just looking for some quick, easy sex. Is that what you think?''

There was pain as well as anger in his terse question, and Caroline's denial held a shocked note. ''Of course that's not what I'm thinking!''

Both anger and confusion mingled in his eyes. ''Then what the hell are you talking about?''

''I know this isn't a deliberate ploy to get me into bed,'' she explained shyly, her face flushing a delicate rose at the intimacy of their conversation. ''You're not the kind of man who would take advantage of a woman's weakness to gain your own ends, no matter what the provocation. But I have provoked your compassion, James. I'm only trying to make you realize that unusual circumstances have colored your attitude toward me. If we'd met in a conventional way, you wouldn't have looked twice at me."

"You're wrong," he drawled huskily as he ran a burning glance across the pale flesh exposed by the open collar of his robe. "Once could never be enough with you."

The double meaning was obvious, and Caroline nervously drew together the edges of the robe with a shaking hand. Clearing her throat, she pleaded, "I wish you wouldn't do that."

One corner of his mouth deepened in the beginning of a smile. "Do what?" he asked in a chiding whisper.

"Look at me that way."

His dark eyebrows rose in a wicked slant, which perfectly complemented the curve of his mouth. "If you prefer, I could close my eyes and touch you instead."

Her expression accusing, she muttered, "You're getting a great deal of enjoyment out of embarrassing me, aren't you?"

"I love to see that peach flush spread across your creamy skin, but I'm not deliberately trying to cause you embarrassment. I want you to be comfortable with me."

She acknowledged the sincerity in his voice, but had to stifle a hysterical urge to laugh. Her eyes were alight with wry self-awareness as she shook her head. "This time your wish isn't going to be granted, James. I'm about as comfortable around you as I'd be if I were sitting on a time bomb.''

"Yes, we do react to each other rather explosively," he murmured throatily. "What are we going to do about it?''

His question caused Caroline's features to tighten with wary defensiveness. "What do you suggest?" she managed, the marked belligerence of her attitude reminding James of a furiously spitting kitten.

"Easy does it, Angel Face."

She gave him a look filled with apprehension, and his momentary amusement disappeared with the rapidity of a mist in a snowstorm. Earlier his hand had shifted to her shoulder, and now he gripped the delicate bones beneath her rounded flesh with almost painful force. His mouth was set in a grim line as he studied her averted profile. "I know I'm moving too damn fast with you, but you're not leaving me much choice."

Caroline's eyes were wide and her expression startled as she jerked her head around to look at him. Her voice registered her indignation as she retorted, "I'm not leaving you much choice? You're the one who…"

"I'm the one who's going slowly out of his mind, Caroline. Don't you think I can understand and sympathize with your dilemma? You've been thrown over for another woman, and you're a mass of doubts and insecurities at the moment. But I'm not faring much better, and I can't allow you to let your logical reservations destroy our relationship before you've given it a chance.''

She sighed with exasperation and shook her head. ''We have no relationship.''

His mouth compressed with grim purpose. ''We have something more important than a knowledge of each other gained by time and proximity. Can't you feel the magic?''

''I'm logical-minded, remember?'' The question was evasive as she tried, with the last of her flagging resistance, to withstand the appeal in his eyes.

His voice was a deep honey drawl as he asked, ''But you feel it, too, don't you? Don't you, Caroline?''

Trapped by the intensity of his melting gaze, the thought of denial never even entered her mind. ''Yes,'' she whispered faintly. ''Yes, I can feel the magic.''

''But?'' he added, immediately sensitive to the slight hesitancy in her manner.

''But magic isn't real,'' she remarked sadly, her eyes green pools of doubt. ''A relationship can't be built on illusion, James. Somewhere along the line reality will destroy the fantasy, and we'll be left with only the knowledge of how naively, how stupidly we've behaved. That's a sure recipe for disaster, and I, for one, am not looking for a new way to inflict more pain on myself.''

''I was naive when I married a woman who only wanted to use me to get to the top in her profession,'' he retorted harshly. ''And I've stupidly wasted the years since by forming unsatisfactory relationships with other females cut from the same cloth as my ex. I couldn't risk being disillusioned again, so it was a case of 'better the devil I knew' than one I didn't.''

"Then don't let me be the one to disillusion you," Caroline pleaded, twisting her hands in her lap. "I don't even know who I am anymore. I wonder now if I ever did."

As he watched the agitated movement of her fingers, his expression filled with something closely resembling anguish. His soft southern drawl was more pronounced than ever when he shifted his attention to her distressed features and said, "That philosophy doesn't apply to you. How could it, when you're as real as a sunrise after a cold, dark night."

Pleasure shivered through her at the flattering comparison, but it was a pleasure tempered with the pain of insecurity. "In a few days you won't even remember what I looked like."

"And will you forget me, sweet Caroline?"

The whispered question made her realize the full extent of her own vulnerability, and she began to shake like an aspen in the wind. "No," she murmured in a dazed certainty. "No, I'll never forget you, James."

His features softened, and he brushed a kiss against the corner of her mouth. "I'll never let you forget."

Another kiss followed the first, and then another, each more poignantly sweet than the last. Soon every inch of her face knew the tender tracing of his lips, and she quivered in his hold like a trapped bird. "This is wrong."

"What's so wrong about two lonely people reaching out for each other, sweetheart?"

Caroline's mind went blank as she tried to think of an answer, and she became panicky at her inability to respond. She nearly groaned at the sensation of that caressing hand against her face, and her voice became a timorous sigh as she grasped at a single straw. "We don't even know each other."

"Do you want to know me?" When she didn't reply, he bent his head until his coffee-scented breath wafted against her lips. "Do you, Caroline?"

"As . . . as in the biblical sense?" she asked, failing to sound as scornful as she'd intended.

His own lips parted as he stared at her mouth. "In every way there is."

"I'm not into one-night stands," she informed him indignantly.

He smiled into eyes he knew were made enormous by nervousness and excitement. "That's good, because I want more than one night with you."

"I don't think—"

"This time I'm glad you're not thinking."

James pressed a kiss against her forehead, and another against the edge of her tip-tilted little nose. His fingers slid under her neck and tangled in the soft curls at her nape. "I've wanted to do this since the moment I first saw you," he whispered hungrily. "Open your mouth for me, Caroline."

Perversely she clamped her mouth closed, but that didn't deter him. With infinite patience he nibbled and licked at her tingling skin, his tongue tracing the fullness of her bottom lip with skillful enjoyment. Caroline heard a buzzing in her ears, and liquid heat flowed from his kiss until she could feel it over every inch of her body. She couldn't seem to gather enough energy to push him away. All her hands seemed to want to do was cling...and cling. Amazing, she thought in bemusement as she gave herself over to a depth of passion she'd never known before. Quite beautiful, wonderful, erotically amazing!

James felt each individual beat of his heart as it pumped the blood searingly through his veins.

His instant arousal was so forceful that he was afraid he might lose control. And *this* was a woman who saw herself as unattractive and boring? he thought incredulously. If she got any more exciting, he'd burst.

He hadn't been excited this quickly or thoroughly since he was a teenager, but was mature enough to control the violence of his response to her. Caroline needed a gentle wooing, and he wanted her satisfaction more than he wanted his own. Because she doubted her femininity, she needed a man who could tap the depths of her sensuality. She needed words of praise and a body hungry for her own. She needed him, he realized with a sigh of pleasure. She needed him!

Caroline had reached the same conclusion. She had no idea why or how it had happened, but she was aware of needing this man with an intensity that both shocked and delighted her. Uttering a small moan, she lifted her hands until they rested against his broad chest. Her fingers curled tentatively, embedding themselves against the softness of his sweater. A masculine growl vibrated against her clinging lips, and a bold tongue demanded entry to the inner warmth of her mouth. Each nerve ending in her body leaped in response, and with sweet willingness she gave him all that he asked of her.

Pulling back from the parted temptation of her mouth, James whispered, "Take my sweater off. I want to feel your hands on me."

Caroline's eyes were hazed with desire as she looked at him, but there was no indecision in the fingers that slowly began to ease the soft fabric over his back and shoulders. With a last tug she pulled the garment over his head and dropped it to the floor beside them. The sweater lay pooled against the pale green carpet, its bunched folds an emphatic statement showing Caroline how far she'd come in so little time. She was finally ready to acknowledge just how badly she wanted this man seated so tensely beside her.

With a tremulous gaze she looked away from the floor to the male perfection of his body. Her breath caught in her throat. Muscles corded the sleek, sunkissed flesh of his arms and shoulders, and a curly trace of dark hair covered his breastbone, tapering into a V that disappeared beneath the waistband of his snugly fitting jeans.

With a trembling hand James brushed moist curls from her temple and huskily encouraged, "Go ahead and touch me, Caroline. Learn the shape and texture of my body, and let me learn yours."

As though in a daze Caroline complied, her fingers slowly drifting across his shoulders, pausing briefly to press against the rapid pulse that was beating in his throat. They continued downward to where dark nipples were peaked in arousal. With a compulsive eagerness that would have shocked her if she'd taken the time to analyze it, she leaned forward and placed her mouth against the warmth of his chest.

Savoring the crisp softness of the dark matt covering his upper body, she inhaled the musky scent that was uniquely James. "You are so beautiful," she whispered.

James felt the words feather on a soft breath against his heated skin, and suddenly had difficulty drawing air into his lungs. The pounding in his chest was suffocatingly swift, and a fine sheen of perspiration seeped through his pores as he gazed down at the dusky curls that tangled and blended with his body hair. He felt the primeval urge of the savage male intent on claiming his mate, and it took all of his willpower to overcome it.

Mistaking the stiffening of his body, Caroline drew back and looked up at him with shy uncertainty. "Did I do something wrong?"

The breath James had been holding shuddered from his lungs, and his smile was strained as he shook his head. "You did something very, very right."

Still not reassured, a tiny frown pleated her brows. "Was it what I said?"

He stared at her mouth in total preoccupation, his attitude vague and his voice distracted as he asked, "What you said?"

Caroline's lips throbbed and softened under the impact of that heated gaze, and she swallowed to ease the dryness that was restricting her throat. "S-some men would be offended by being called beautiful."

His eyes shot to hers, an incredulous expression in their depths. "You don't really believe that."

"It is a rather...effeminate phrase."

"It might seem that way to a man who has doubts about his own masculinity, but I'm pleased that you find my body beautiful."

James paused, then carefully reached out to gently circle her wrists with his long fingers. Tugging with unspoken purpose, he drew her hands to his chest and began rotating her palms against his skin in an evocative circular motion. In a voice thickened by desire, he murmured, "Can't you tell how much it pleases me to have you touch me? Do you like the feel of your hands on my body as much as I do, Caroline?"

"Oh, yes," she sighed, fascinated by the sight of her paler flesh against his warm, olive-skinned body. Her features alight with curiosity now, she curled her fingers until her nails were scraping against him. He jerked in involuntary reaction, and Caroline's gaze widened with the knowledge of Eve. "Do you like that?"

His voice a barely recognizable throaty growl, he rasped, "You know I do, but I'd like it a lot more if I could return the favor."

With an assumption of casualness he was far from feeling, James hooked his thumbs around the lapels of her robe. Inch by inch the material parted and his eyes filled with anticipation as he savored the moment to the fullest. Full creamy mounds, their pink-tinted crests hardened with arousal, were exposed to his appreciative gaze. "So lovely," he murmured thickly, "so damn lovely."

Unable to resist temptation for a second longer, James bent his head and flicked his tongue over a pouting tip. When Caroline arched her back and cried out, a teasing smile etched the corners of his mobile mouth. In a voice laden with sensuality he repeated her earlier question. "Do you like that?"

Submerged beneath his fiery gaze, Caroline's thoughts scattered like leaves on the wind. From the top of her head to the tips of her toes she was awash with sensation. She was burning with a slow fire that was building inside her, leaving her trembling and aching in its wake.

"You do like it, don't you?" James whispered, confident enough of himself to know the answer without being told. With a laugh of pure masculine triumph, he buried his mouth against her throat. His hands lifted and cupped her breasts with a tenderness that amounted to near reverence.

"Sweet heaven, you make me ache like a boy with his first woman. You're so sweet, so honey sweet. I've never felt like this in my life before. From the moment I first saw you, it was as though you'd crawled inside my skin and become a part of me. Let me love you, my honey. Please let me become a part of you."

With a gentle hesitancy that caught at Caroline's heart, he reached out and tugged at the tie belt still circling her waist. The folds of the robe parted, completely revealing her lush nakedness. The expression on his face as he looked down at her was a revelation, easing any awkwardness she might have felt as he urged her to lie against the welcoming cushions of the sofa. A surge of joy pierced Caroline at the look of wonder in his eyes, and any remaining self-consciousness fled before the force of his masculine appraisal.

James's chest rose and fell with mesmerizing rapidity as he struggled to breath naturally. A flush of arousal had darkened his broad cheekbones. He shook his head in an attempt to clear his passion-dazed mind. His sable-hued hair tumbled across his forehead, obscuring that betraying hint of passionate dew from Caroline's fascinated gaze. In a gesture as natural as breathing, she reached up and brushed the soft, unruly locks back into place.

As though galvanized into action by the unpremeditated tenderness of the gesture, James lost the battle he'd been waging with his self-control. He wanted her naked and yielding beneath him, the need to bury himself in her warmth superseding every sane thought in his head. A groan erupted from his parted lips, and his eyes flashed a wild message as he yanked the robe off her shoulders and down her arms.

He knew by the sudden tensing of her body that he was going too fast for Caroline, but couldn't seem to stop himself. When she uttered a startled murmur of protest, he drowned the incomprehensible sound with his voraciously hungry mouth. The hands she pressed against his chest were more of a warm inducement than a deterrent, and he quickly lowered himself on top of her trembling body.

James shifted until his aching male flesh was cradled between the valley of her thighs. Only the painfully tight material of his jeans prevented the joining he longed for, and the knowledge of just how temporary a barrier it presented was nearly driving him out of his mind. He groaned and pressed his damp forehead against the scented flesh of her breasts in a curiously vulnerable gesture.

"I'm sorry," he cried out in torment. "Don't let me frighten you, Caroline."

His plea was accompanied by a convulsive rocking motion of his hips, but oddly enough Caroline's apprehension was eased by his lack of control. "It's all right," she murmured gently, cradling his head in her arms. "I'm not afraid of you, only of what's happening to me."

Her admission pierced his passion-induced preoccupation, and he braced his weight on his elbows until he was able to meet her eyes. The sensual glow in their forest-green depths nearly stopped his breathing, and his own expression was filled with dazed incredulity as he whispered, "It's happening to both of us, darlin'."

"We barely know each other, and yet we..."

She clenched her teeth, and he rubbed his thumb against her rigid jawline in a soothing gesture. "We what, sweet?"

"We burn together," she murmured faintly.

Heat flooded his loins at her honesty, but the relief he felt at her admission was greater than his physical reaction. To know that she was as trapped in passion's inferno as he was gave him hope for the future...a future with Caroline. "Is that how you feel?" he questioned, vaguely ashamed of his need for added reassurance. "Are you burning for me?"

Caroline was stunned by the flicker of uncertainty she glimpsed in his eyes. That she could cause a man as strong and forceful and intrinsically confident as James to expose such a depth of vulnerability awed her, and flooded her entire being with tender compassion. A smile trembled on her mouth as she whispered, "Yes. I'm on fire for you, James."

With a strangled groan that merged relief with triumph, James hungrily captured her smile with his lips and claimed it for his own. Caroline needed no urging to open her mouth, accepting the fiery thrust of his tongue with an eagerness no longer shadowed with doubt. Her hands slid around his back to pull him closer, and she marvelled at the pleasure she felt as her open palms grazed his warm flesh.

That pleasure was intensified a thousandfold when his fingers began to glide against the hardened peak of her breast. When she arched her back their mouths were wrenched apart, but James gave her no time to mourn the loss. Instantly he lowered his head and engulfed her throbbing nipple in his mouth, his groan of satisfaction blending with her own. The hand that kneaded and caressed the surrounding flesh was gentle yet insistent. The rhythmic undulations of his hips matched the heated suckling of his mouth, and with a tiny gasp of frustration Caroline lifted her own hips to seek closer contact.

James cried out as her feminine heat penetrated his clothing, every muscle in his body clenching in protest as he lifted himself away from her. "James?" she murmured faintly in protest.

He rose to his feet and his trembling fingers fumbled with the snap and zipper of his jeans, while his dark eyes blazed down at her with golden sparks in their depths. "I can't hold back any longer," he ground out through gritted teeth. "It has to be now, Caroline!"

His voice was harsh with demand, but there was an unspoken plea underlying the passion in his intense gaze. Once again she was witnessing the vulnerability he couldn't hide, and her arms reached out to him with a hunger to match his own. "Make love to me, James."

The time that followed was more magical than either of them had imagined possible. Caroline responded mindlessly to his avid exploration of her flesh, her hands journeying on their own path of discovery as she shivered in his arms. By the time James filled her body with his hard, driving strength, Caroline's brain was already exploding with sensations too exquisite to be withstood for long. Gasping his name, she arched beneath him in an agony of fulfillment.

"Yes, love," he muttered against her throat. "Burn for me . . . like I'm burning for you!"

Then with a final, violent surge of his hips James was joining her in the conflagration, and they clung to each other like storm-tossed ships on a raging sea. Caroline held him tightly as their pulsing heartbeats slowed to a normal rhythm, needing the warm reassurance of his body as she tried to comprehend the miracle she'd just experienced. She wasn't frigid, she realized, the knowledge causing tears of relief to slip from beneath her closed eyelids. She had never been frigid!

James shifted to his side, and cradled Caroline's body in his arms. As he lifted his head to kiss her, he noticed the moisture trailing down her cheeks. Alarm ripped through him, his voice holding a note of fear as he cried, "Caroline, are you all right? Did I hurt you?"

Her lashes fluttered briefly, then rose to inspect his concerned features. She bit down on her lip, which was red and swollen from the force of his kisses. Wincing more from the thoughts tumbling around in her head than from the bruised sensitivity of her mouth, she responded to his comment with a disbelieving shake of her head. "I just feel . . . cheated, James."

Pain exploded behind his eyes, and with an apologetic murmur she placed her fingertips against his mouth before he could protest her callous words. "No, you don't understand," she explained hurriedly. "I didn't mean that the way it sounded, but for years I've blamed myself for being a sexual misfit. I'd defend myself from Frank's accusations by accusing him of failing me, but deep down inside I believed him.

"It was so different with you," she whispered in awe. "You were concerned with pleasing me . . . so sweet and caring. You've given me a confidence in myself as a woman I've never had before, because now I can finally accept the truth. Frank really was too self-centered to do anything but take his own pleasure at my expense, wasn't he?"

His mouth curved into an indulgent smile. "I'm only glad that you're able to see that now, Caroline. You're a warm, sensual woman with a great deal to give any man. Don't ever doubt that, darlin'."

"You really did know that all along, didn't you?"

"I knew," he whispered.

Caroline had to swallow hard before she could speak the single word her brain had formed. "How?"

"Because of the magic," he said huskily. "It's as real as we are, honey sweet."

"How can you be so certain?"

His smile now held indulgence as well as pleasure. "The moment I saw you I began to believe, with everything I am or ever hope to be."

With a relieved sigh Caroline linked her hands together behind his neck, her expression solemn as she gazed up at him. "I wish I could be certain that the magic won't just disappear, James."

Slowly he got to his feet and leaned down to lift her against his chest. He brushed his mouth against the top of her head as he carried her toward the curved stairs leading to his bedroom. As he began the ascent, Caroline hid her face against his throat with a choked murmur of relief.

"This is the first time I've ever held this kind of magic in my arms, but I know it won't fade away, love," he assured her, his voice shaking with emotion. "Not if we teach each other to trust in what we've found."

Five

Caroline was not an early-morning person under the best of circumstances. She was an individual who needed a full eight to ten hours of sleep before she could get her motor running and last night she had barely slept at all. When she opened her eyes to the twilight hours just before dawn, she was amazed at the clarity of her mind. She remembered everything that had happened to her before she'd fallen into an exhausted slumber—and wished to God she didn't.

She remembered the cool feel of silken sheets against her naked skin; the warm, sensitive fingers that had explored her body until she writhed beneath the massive shadow the man cast over her like a thing gone wild and the scents that had mingled in the air as they made love. She remembered a mouth skilled in all the ways a woman values most and the husky murmurs of pleasure and praise breathed into her ear. She remembered her own cries as she was transported beyond pleasure to ecstasy, not once but innumerable times during those enchanted hours. She remembered too much—and wanted to forget.

The magic had fled, as she had known it would, and she was left aching in both body and soul as the rain-laden sky lightened beyond the window. Shadows entered the room to mingle with those in her heart, as she lay stiff and cold beside the man who still held her as he slept. With an awkward movement she shifted her head until she could look over her shoulder, and her heart nearly stopped as she studied her lover's bold, masculine features.

Her lover! Such a simple description, and yet those words had forever shattered her own conception of herself. She had let herself be picked up and taken home by a stranger, and she had ended up in his bed. Those facts were irrefutable, and no amount of soul-searching was going to make any difference. How could it, when she was totally responsible for the mess she found herself in? Caroline Barclay had not only fallen from grace, she thought cynically, she had plunged over the cliff with all the enthusiasm of a trained diver.

She tried to tell herself she'd been upset and not thinking with her usual degree of clarity last night, yet it didn't do her conscience the least bit of good. She

could excuse her behavior but never could she con-
done it. She glanced down at her hand, which was
clutching the edge of the silky sheet with white-
knuckled desperation. There was a deep indentation
on the finger where her wedding ring used to be, and
an intense feeling of shame coursed through her.
Closing her eyes, she forced back the tears that
threatened to destroy any remaining composure. Then
she tried to decide what she should do now.

One thing was certain; she was going to get out of
here before James awakened. There was no way she
could contemplate the thought of facing those all-
seeing eyes of his in the morning light. He, too, would
remember the way she'd responded to his heated kisses
and gentle touch. The memory of her abandoned behavior would be there when he looked at her, and she
couldn't bear it.

Had she really been that sensually demanding
woman or was it some figment of her imagination?
Had she really given him the intensity of pleasure his
shuddering body had indicated, or had she been
dreaming? Caroline inwardly flinched at the questions she didn't want answered. There was no time for
any more soul-searching, not if she wanted to escape
before the man who had gained such intimate knowledge of her awakened.

Their night of magic was over, and now it was time
for her to yield to reality. Returning to her normal life-
style without coming to terms with what had happened last night was a mistake, but it was the only path

open to her. She would just have to suffer the guilt and embarrassment that was the bitter residue of her irrational behavior.

James didn't belong to her world, and she didn't want to belong to his. One man had brought her to this low ebb in her life, she thought bitterly, and she certainly didn't need another one now. If she'd learned one thing during the past hours, it was that she'd never really discovered who she was. She had to unravel the person trapped inside the functioning shell she'd been all these years, before she could share that person with anyone else.

Slowly she lifted the heavy, hair-roughened arm from around her waist, catching her breath when James muttered something in his sleep and rolled onto his back. Caroline slowly eased herself off the mattress. Cool air struck her naked flesh and she shivered. She avoided looking at the splendid, sprawling male figure in the bed, too afraid that she might not be able to leave him if she did.

The recognition of her own weakness had her scurrying from the room and down the darkened stairway with more speed than grace. Luckily the thickness of the carpeting muffled her flight, and she burst into the living room feeling rather like a hunted creature. Frantically she searched the shadows for her clothes, subduing a frustrated groan when she remembered they'd never been taken out of the dryer. Instead she stared at the robe crumpled in artless abandon against the cushioned sofa, and felt the heat in her cheeks increase a hundredfold.

She had to search for the utility room, which she found off the kitchen. She stood on the cold linoleum tile beside the washer and dryer, her bare feet frozen as she pulled on her wrinkled garments. Once dressed she felt marginally better, and paused long enough to run shaking hands through her disordered hair. Taking a deep breath while firmly ordering herself to relax, she slid her still-damp shoes onto her feet and tiptoed to the kitchen door. Sliding it open, she escaped into the misty dawn.

James tore down the stairs with the roar of a wounded lion. Rain still dripped down the wall of glass facing him, but the sun was finally winning its battle with the storm. Although muted, the late-morning sunlight cast a golden reflection upon his nakedness. But there was no warmth for him in the new day, and with a muttered invective he grabbed his robe from the couch and put it on. It smelled of Caroline, and he closed his eyes in an agony of regret.

The magic hadn't been strong enough to hold her, he thought dully. While he was weak and vulnerable in sleep, she had broken free of the charmed circle and disappeared into the real world she prized so highly. James's hand tightened into a fist, and he slammed it against his thigh in frustrated anger. What in the hell was he going to do now?

Walking toward the plate-glass window that over-looked the river, he leaned his forehead against the cool surface. As he watched the water trickle down the glass, he felt a loneliness more acute than anything he'd ever experienced. He pictured Caroline in his mind, and remembered the way she'd flowed over and around and through him like the sweet honey he'd compared her to. She had warmed his soul with the generosity of her spirit, and now he was colder than a man should ever have to be.

A terrible sensation of loss invaded the emptiness inside him, and he closed his eyes against the pain. It was as if a part of himself had been ripped away, a part vital to his existence. He didn't even know her last name, he realized with a sensation of gut-wrenching fear. But she was somewhere out there, and he'd find her if it was the last thing he ever did.

He would find her, and neither of them would be lonely again. He'd reweave the magic fabric that had drawn them together, until it was strong enough to withstand the pressures of the real world. That goal was a shining promise in his heart, a sacred vow for the future. James's chest rose on a calming breath, and his lashes lifted to reveal eyes dark with purpose. Then Caroline would know what he had accepted from the beginning . . . that they belonged together and always would.

"Rise and shine, Mother mine!"

The lump under the blankets stirred and uttered a

word she wouldn't dream of letting her son use. "Go 'way!"

Caroline heard the sound of the draperies being drawn and scooted farther under the covers. She loved her sole offspring, but he was a morning person and she hated morning people. He was even whistling, for heaven's sake! How anyone could sound so cheerful this early in the day was a complete mystery to her, especially one who'd been out partying the night before. That reminded her of the little talk she intended having with Pete, and she wriggled with irritation as her maternal conscience pierced the fog embedded so comfortably in her brain.

Fingers plucked repeatedly at the bedspread. "Come out, come out, wherever you are."

"You're playing a dangerous game, my son."

"What?" he yelled with exaggerated exuberance, a thread of laughter accompanying the word. "Are you really alive and well under there? That's good, because your coffee's getting cold."

"That's dirty pool," she mumbled resentfully.

"I've had years of practice," he replied, pulling a corner of the sheet aside as he searched for a face to go with the disembodied voice. "Are you coming out, or should I dial 911 to have you rescued?"

Caroline sniffed, first disdainfully, then with more appreciation. The coffee smelled heavenly and was the one inducement guaranteed to get her out of bed. There was no way she was going to go back to sleep with that aroma tantalizing her nostrils, and she gave a sigh of disgruntled resignation as she began fighting free of the bedclothes.

She managed to prop both herself and her pillow against the headboard and reached out blindly with one hand. She knew the shape and the feel of her favorite mug, and her fingers curled eagerly around the handle. "Thanks," she said with belated politeness. "What time is it?"

Her question was deliberately misinterpreted. "It's time to open your eyes."

Cautiously she lifted her right eyelid, and a dancing prism of light caught her squarely on the pupil. She winced, adding sunlight to her list of pet peeves. "No, it's not."

Pete leaned forward and gave her an encouraging smile. "Come on, you're halfway there."

"I'm halfway alive, but that doesn't matter to you in the least, you coldhearted monster child."

"I'm only trying to save you from yourself," the monster child retorted with disgusting cheerfulness. "You don't want to go through life looking like Popeye, do you?"

Her other eyelid joined the first at half-mast. She gave him one of her sweetest, most deceptive smiles. "What time did you get home last night, Peter?"

"Oops," he uttered with a chagrined grimace. "Is that why you look like you didn't get much sleep?"

Her innate honesty wouldn't allow her to add to his guilt, and she shook her head while stifling a yawn. "No, I made the mistake of going out for coffee after class. When I got home I was too wired to sleep, so I hit the books.''

He grinned sympathetically. ''Your last two finals are this week, aren't they?''

Caroline sipped at the dark, aromatic beverage in her mug and gave an appreciative groan. ''I take it back,'' she sighed fulsomely. ''No monster child could make a cup of coffee this heavenly. And yes, if all goes well, your mother will be a graduate of Smith Technical College by Friday. Then all I'll have to worry about is getting someone to hire me for longer than two weeks.''

Pete plopped onto the edge of the bed and gave her a reproving look. ''You don't have to worry about a thing and you know it. Since Dad walked out, you've nearly killed yourself working temporary jobs during the day and going to school evenings. It's been a tough seven months, but you've made it. In case I haven't told you this before, I'm damn proud of you!''

Caroline looked into blue eyes filled with pride and approval. Tears blurred her vision. In a voice choked with emotion she admitted, ''I couldn't have made it without you, love.''

His grin held the winsome appeal of a little boy secure in his mother's affections, and the cockiness of a young man confident of his place in the world. ''I was taught never to argue with my elders, especially when I'm already in hot water.''

Reminded of her maternal duties, she gave him her sternest ''I am your mother'' look. ''You have a one o'clock curfew on the weekends, but might I remind you that today is only Thursday, and—'' Caroline let out a screech of dismay, her eyes rounded in horrified realization ''—and I've got an interview for a job this morning!''

Pete calmly extricated the coffee mug from certain disaster and gave her a soothing smile. ''It's only seven-thirty. You've got plenty of time.''

Her mouth formed a tiny moue of dismay as she stared at the green digital numbers on her bedside clock radio. ''Seven-thirty?'' she squeaked in disbelief. ''No wonder I feel as though I'd just shut my eyes.''

Scrambling over the side of the bed with more haste than grace, Caroline hit the floor at a run. Pausing only long enough to peck her son on the cheek, she scurried toward the open bathroom door. Pete watched the hem of his old blue-and-gold football jersey flap around his mother's knees. Her hair was sticking out in wiry curls all over her head, her arms were flapping like the wings of an agitated chicken, and she was talking to herself.

Laughing beneath his breath, he called out, ''Hey, Mom, don't you want to know why I was late last night?''

''I'm sure you had a good reason, Pete.''

''A few of the guys were a little the worse for wear, so I drove them home.''

When there was only a distracted, if approving, mutter from behind the bathroom door, Pete's smile widened and the expression in his eyes grew softly indulgent. Because they shared a relationship based on mutual trust and respect, he had known there would be no anger or reproach for his late night. He didn't often break the rules, mainly because he knew Caroline worried herself into a frazzle whenever he was late getting home. But no matter how worried she grew, she always gave him the benefit of the doubt. He only wished she had as much faith in herself as she did in him, but she was getting there. She was one in a million, that mother of his. The only problem was convincing her of that.

"Caroline, I'm really hesitant about sending you out on this particular job interview." Linda Avery, of Avery's Employment Services, tapped a long, manicured fingernail against the file on her desk. "Mr. Mitchel has proven to be one of our more difficult customers. He's gone through four temps in as many months, and all of them have threatened to commit mayhem on my person if I ever even dream of asking them to go back. If the man didn't pay so well I'd drop him from our list, but he offers an incentive bonus that my avaricious heart just can't resist."

Caroline gave a gurgle of laughter and eyed her employer fondly. Anyone less mercenary than the buxom, gray-haired woman in front of her would be hard to find. Linda was always willing to champion the underdog, and Caroline herself was a prime example. Six months ago she'd desperately needed work to supplement the support payments from Frank, but no one had been willing to hire a woman with only meager high-school typing skills and no work record.

Then she had walked through the doors of this ultramodern office with its plate-glass windows and metal filing cabinets, tired, dispirited, and very much on the defensive. But Linda Avery had not only listened to her tale of woe, she had immediately given her a job to go to. Admittedly those first assignments had taxed Caroline's physical stamina more than her intellectual ability, but they had done a great deal to build her self-confidence. Night school had accomplished the rest, and as her skills grew, so had the quality of the jobs Linda had sent her on.

Proud of the confidence her employer had in her, Caroline attempted to reassure the other woman. "I'm a survivor, Linda. You know I can take whatever your Mr. Mitchel dishes out."

Giving her a fond glance Linda said, "You've proven your worth to this agency many times over, honey, but that doesn't mean I have the right to throw you to the wolves. Loyalty should be rewarded, not punished. The word has gotten out on this particular canine, and the girls who aren't already on assignment have turned me down flat. You have that same right."

"If I choose to exercise it," Caroline agreed with a smile, "which I don't. Now, where is this particular lair, and what will my duties consist of?"

Linda hesitated before withdrawing a slip of paper from the file. Handing it to Caroline, she gave her a rueful grin. "I knew you'd look on this assignment as a challenge, which makes me feel as guilty as sin. But you just remember that you're free to walk out of there if the beast puts too much pressure on you. I won't have any of my girls developing an ulcer because of a job I've sent them to. It would raise my insurance premiums."

Chuckling at this latest falsehood, Caroline glanced down at the paper in her hand. Immediately her eyes widened and began to sparkle with excitement. "I'll be working as personal secretary to the editor of the *Sacramento News*?" she asked breathlessly.

"The owner and editor," Linda added grumpily. "Mr. Mitchel wields a great deal of power and influence in this town, which is why his patronage is such a feather in my agency's cap."

"I won't let you down, Linda."

"You just get that groupie grin off your face and listen, Caroline. I can tell by your expression that you like the idea of working for a newspaper, but so did the other girls I sent there. They soon found out the job wasn't all it was cracked up to be. According to them, Mitchel expects more of a girl Friday and general dogsbody than anything else. From the things I've heard about him from other sources, the man's a workaholic and as tough as old boots. He's scrupulously fair and honest, but he demands the same dedication and single-mindedness from his employees as he gives to that paper himself. It might say 'nine to five' under the job description, but don't you believe it!''

"With Pete starting college in the fall, I can use all the overtime I can get," Caroline responded happily, not one whit discouraged by Linda's gloomy predictions. "Is there a chance of this position becoming permanent?"

Nodding resignedly, Linda's features took on an even more doleful cast. "I thought that possibility would appeal to you."

"You know I've been happy working for you," Caroline interjected hastily. "It's just that I—"

"You need permanence."

"Yes," she responded softly. "I guess at heart I'm still a homebody with a need for my own personal niche, and that house of mine is going to be an empty shell once Pete is enrolled in college. When I was younger my favorite comic strip character was Lois Lane, and not because she led Superman around by his cape. If I can prove myself to Mr. Mitchel, maybe he'll let me train as a reporter. I'll need something to fill the spaces in my life, Linda."

"I know you will," the other woman agreed gently. "But don't be too disappointed if this doesn't pan out. Even after all you've gone through, you're still so damn trusting and vulnerable, it's unbelievable. You may have quit believing in Superman, but you're still looking for happy endings, honey. I don't want you to feel like a failure if this doesn't work out for you.

You've come a long way in a short time, and I promise you there will be other opportunities."

Linda followed her to the door, and Caroline turned and gave her an impulsive hug. "I'll make it work," she whispered.

As she walked through the reception lounge and exited the outer door, Caroline was unaware of the worried glint in Linda Avery's astute brown eyes.

From the instant she entered the central office of the *Sacramento News*, Caroline was lost. Phones were ringing, computer keyboards were clacking, and the large, barnlike area split into small partitioned cubicles seemed to seethe with constant movement. The atmosphere was noisy, hectic, and held a constant undercurrent of suppressed excitement. The aura of controlled chaos was immensely appealing to a woman like herself, whose life had so far been directed along orderly and individuality-stifling lines.

Since she'd started working as an Avery temp, this was the first time she'd wanted a job badly enough to be nervous. Hesitantly approaching the front desk, she gave her name to the woman on duty. She was greeted by a grin and a breezy, "So you're the newest one to be fed to the lion."

Caroline blinked and a slow smile curved her mouth. "Wolf," she corrected succinctly. "And this time he may discover he's bitten off more than he can chew."

Surprised admiration glinted in the receptionist's dark eyes, and she pursed her lips in a soundless whistle. "It seems Madam Avery has saved her most impressive artillery for the last."

"That she has," Caroline replied demurely, with an air of assurance she only wished she felt. Her prospective boss was beginning to assume the proportions of a bogeyman, which didn't do much to bolster her confidence. She had never had much of that commodity to begin with, and only hoped she could bluff her way through this interview. A deeply drawn breath absorbed the scents from her surroundings, and a tingle of excitement helped to stiffen her spine. She wanted this job, and she was going to get it.

"My name is Consuelo, and this is Jeff," the woman told her, grabbing the arm of a young boy not much older than Pete as he passed her desk. "He's a copy boy and an ace reporter in training, according to him."

Jeff flushed to the roots of his buzzed red hair, his freckled face holding a sheepish expression as he shook Caroline's hand. "Not yet, but I will be soon. Mr. Mitchel's sending me to journalism school in the fall."

"Jeff!" Consuelo squealed, jumping to her feet and throwing her arms around the startled boy. "That's terrific! When did you find out?"

"This morning when I delivered his mail," he replied shyly. "I told him my family couldn't afford to send me, but he said he'd foot the bills. I still can't believe it. Mr. Mitchel is sure a terrific guy!''

''That's what I was just going to tell our new associate here,'' Consuelo retorted with a grin in Caroline's direction. ''The boss snaps and snarls a bit, but underneath all the bluster he's a marshmallow. Don't let him scare you off like the others, Caroline.''

Jeff's bushy eyebrows rose. ''She's the new secretary?''

''If he hires me,'' Caroline responded nervously. ''I still have to get through the interview in one piece.''

''Then the sooner you get it over with, the better,'' Jeff replied cheerfully, gesturing for Caroline to follow him. ''Come on, let's go beard the lion in his den.''

''Wolf,'' Caroline corrected faintly, her eyes wide with apprehension as she followed Jeff across the room.

Everyone's attention seemed to be trained on the middle of her back as she passed, and she only prayed they wouldn't notice the way her knees were knocking. Wiping the damp palms against the side of her tailored navy-blue skirt, she gave Jeff a strained smile when he turned to check her progress.

''Here you go,'' he said, stopping in front of a door bearing a metal placard with raised black letters spelling the word Editor. ''Just give a knock and go in. The boss doesn't insist on formality.''

With a wave and a murmured, ''Good luck,'' Jeff was loping back the way he'd come and Caroline was standing alone in a state of near panic. Glancing over her shoulder at all the staring faces, she moistened her dry lips with the tip of her tongue. The other women seemed to be wearing jeans and casual lightweight tops. For that matter, so did the men.

She felt distinctly overdressed in her suit and tailored white blouse. But before she could use that as an excuse to run for the hills, she reminded herself that she was appropriately attired for an interview. Turning to face the door, she tilted her chin with determination and rapped firmly on the wooden surface. A voice responded with a surly admonition to enter, and Caroline stepped forward to meet her uncertain fate.

Six

Caroline's eyes were lowered as she entered the room and turned to close the door behind her. After the cacophony of sound she'd left behind her, the sudden quiet grated on her nerves, which weren't in the best condition to begin with. Swallowing to assure herself that she still could, she fixed a plastic smile on her face and pivoted on her high heels. She had actually taken a couple of steps forward when a voice ripped through the silence with enough force to shake the plaster off the pale gold walls.

"Caroline!"

Shocked nearly senseless, she struggled to catch her breath. Ordinarily she would have paid more attention to the walnut-grained beauty of the massive desk

and matching file cabinets, and the intricate work-
manship of the stately grandfather clock against the
far wall. She appreciated fine furniture and knew
quality when she saw it, even if she could rarely afford the price. But in that instant her attention was
fixed solely on the tense figure framed by the sunlight, which poured in through the bay window behind him.

Caroline's mouth opened in disbelief as she stared
at the man she had thought never to see again. Thick,
tobacco-brown hair with a tendency toward unruli-
ness; sun-bronzed skin; dark eyes rimmed by an am-
ber glow. She didn't know if he was real, or a
hallucination brought on by stress. She didn't know if
the sound thudding in her ears was coming from her
pounding heart or her knocking knees. All she knew
for certain was that every muscle in her body, with the
exception of those damn knees, was frozen solid.

"James," she managed finally. "How nice to see
you again."

She closed her eyes on a disgusted breath, unable to
believe she'd really uttered that inane platitude. When
she remembered the way he'd last seen her, sprawled
naked against his big body, she wondered if a person
could actually die of embarrassment. If so, she was
well on the way to being delivered to the pearly gates,
although with the kind of thoughts skittering around
in her brain, she sure as shooting wasn't going to be
allowed to get past them into heaven. She could almost hear them clanging shut on her arrival!

No, it was the discordant squeak of James's chair she was hearing, and her eyes popped open in self-defense as he jumped to his feet and came toward her. There was a ferocious scowl on his face and his large frame held almost visibly leashed tension. The golden flecks in his brown eyes had kindled into leaping fires. His mouth was a taut, straight slash denoting barely suppressed rage.

"It sure as hell took you long enough, woman! Do you know what you've put me through?"

Caroline blinked at him in confusion. Good Lord, she'd forgotten how enormous he was! She tried to melt into the solid surface at her back, but the wood remained rigidly uncooperative. James was bearing down on her like an eighteen-wheeler on a steep grade, and if his expression was anything to go by, he had no intention of putting on his brakes. Certain the breath she sucked into her lungs would be her last, she waited for the inevitable collision.

When it came it wasn't with a force to promote fear, but was instead a seductive pressure that caused every nerve end in her body to jangle into riotous life. His hot, overpowering male frame pressed against her with fervent power, and she was enveloped in an embrace that felt like a homecoming. Languidly she lowered her lashes to let them rest against her flushed cheeks, while all her senses concentrated on remembering.

The spicy odor of the soap he favored blended with that of his lemony after-shave, but it was the musky, uniquely pleasurable scent of his body that caught at her senses. She felt his warmth seeping through her flesh to reignite the fires that had been cold and dead since they'd parted. She listened to the thunder of his heartbeat match the rhythm of her own. She shivered as she remembered responding to him in a similar manner on that night so long ago.

"Oh, how I've missed you."

Caroline's chest tightened as she heard the pain and loneliness in his voice. Yes, she'd missed him, too, but the realization brought her no comfort. For seven months she'd fought her battle with the memories and struggled to establish her own independence. She'd managed to survive, but she had finally been forced to accept the intrinsic weakness beneath the surface strength she projected. She was a woman who needed a man's warmth and approval to complete her, and she had no intention of ever again giving in to that fatal flaw in her character.

"Don't!" she cried, pushing against his chest with hands that held too little strength to be effective. "Please let me go, James."

"You don't mean that." His teeth caught at the lobe of her ear and his hands slid down her arched spine to draw her more forcefully into the cradle of his tight, muscular thighs. "There's no need for coy games, Caroline. You've finally come back to me, that's all that matters."

The husky murmur accomplished what her own willpower couldn't, and she jerked her head back until she was able to meet his eyes. His arrogant assumption had set her temper ablaze, but it was the look of smug satisfaction stamped on his features that caused her fingers to curl against the front of his shirt like claws. "I beg your pardon?"

With a condescending indulgence that made her want to smack him, he grinned down at her. "The only thing you have to beg my pardon for is sneaking out of my bed. It wasn't pleasant to wake up and find you gone. It wasn't pleasant at all. I've nearly gone crazy looking for you all these months."

"You needn't have bothered," she responded frigidly.

Although his lips tightened with annoyance, he continued as though she hadn't spoken. "I contracted with a couple of the best detective agencies in the business to try and track you down, but with only a general description and no last name to give them, they didn't have a lot to go on. They've been checking all the Carolines who have filed for divorce, but none of the ones they've contacted had a teenage son name Peter. I couldn't remember your damned husband's name, and I've gone through hell thinking you may have gone back to him."

"Frank," she murmured weakly.

"What?"

"My husband," she repeated with unconscious defensiveness. "His name is Frank."

He cupped her cheeks in his hands, his eyes tormented. "You haven't, have you?"

She didn't pretend to misunderstand him. "No, we're divorced, but I—"

Bending, he pressed his forehead against hers. "Thank God. I couldn't have taken that, sweetheart."

Caroline pulled away and looked up at him in confusion. "I don't know why you should have gone to so much trouble."

"Why I—?" He stiffened, his face darkening with temper. "You know the answer as well as I do!"

She gave him an exasperated glance and shook her head. "For heaven's sake, I was just a woman you picked up, a—a one-night stand that never should have happened."

"Don't say that," he muttered. "Don't cheapen something so beautiful."

Although she feared giving a man this dominant the upper hand, Caroline couldn't help the healing warmth that flooded through her at his words. She'd had shame as her constant companion for the past seven months, and a part of that hair shirt had been made of imagining what James must think of her. Now she knew. Something solid inside her took a new form, but without the jagged edges she'd become accustomed to.

Softness was reflected on her face and she whispered, "Thank you."

"I should be the one saying that to you," he remarked with a widening grin. "You could have just come by the house, but you went to the trouble of finding out where I worked. I appreciate the extra effort, but not if that's the reason you've left me hanging fire all this time."

Caroline mentally counted to ten, but found that the exercise failed to calm her renewed anger. Were all men this egotistically sure of themselves, she wondered, or had James managed to corner the market? Twisting her head free of his hold, she glared up at him in righteous indignation. "What makes you think I would go to the trouble of looking for you?"

"You're here, aren't you?"

Her eyes flashing emerald fire, she snapped, "For your information, I would not waste my time searching for you or any other man. Just what kind of a woman do you think I am?"

"This office doesn't afford me the kind of privacy I need to answer that question, Caroline." His slumbrous gaze fell to her mouth. "Come home with me and I'll show you what I think."

Caroline felt her heartbeat accelerate as she recalled all the delicious, mind-boggling exercises he could choose from to get his viewpoint across. James had a way of touching a woman that made her feel . . . cherished. She remembered the way his hands had flowed over her body like the whisper of a wild, hot wind, and how he had made her burn for him. As she was burning for him now, she realized, shocked at the sensation of aching warmth.

Caroline felt a swift stab of self-disgust. She was like an empty vessel needing to be filled, a lump of clay prepared to be molded by the sculptor. She was standing here like a mindless idiot, waiting for James's next move as though she had no say in the matter. Her body was wired with exquisite tension as she silently willed him to make that move and free her from any responsibility. I'm like a damn dog listening for his master's command, she decided derisively.

Her thoughts made her weak, and that made her madder than ever. She didn't want her mind boggled, she thought furiously, and the sooner James realized that the better! She was only now discovering herself to be a capable, fully functioning human being, and the threat this man posed to her newfound autonomy made her panic-stricken. He was all bold decisiveness, an indomitable male, and she was as responsive to his forceful appeal as ever.

No matter how attracted she was to James Mitchel, she knew intuitively that he was dangerous to her plans for the future. He was too strong, too powerful, and if the look in his eyes was anything to go by . . . much too possessive and autocratic to be let loose in her life. Eventually he would discover the one weakness that must be kept hidden from him, if she was to have a chance in hell of retaining her independence. Damn it, she wouldn't let herself need him or any other man!

Drawing herself up to her full five foot, six, if she counted her heels, Caroline gave him her sternest look. "I hate to burst your bubble, but I'm here on business, James."

His eyes sparkled with amusement as he took careful note of her militant stance. She was all fire and ruffled indignation. A swift upsurge of desire caught him by surprise. The breath left his lungs in an agonized burst and his mouth parted to draw in necessary oxygen. He wanted Caroline with an urgency that blocked every other thought from his mind, and with a guttural cry he bent and captured her lips with his own.

His tongue sought out her sweet honey and slick, delicious warmth. He felt as well as heard her muffled protest, but he was beyond listening. He was deaf and blind to everything but his hunger for her. In a darting plunge his hands slid downward, stopping only when they reached their goal, filling themselves with the soft flesh of her buttocks, kneading and molding the resilient curves until he felt her body sag against him in capitulation.

But unfortunately for James, Caroline's momentary weakness helped to banish the mists of desire from her brain at last. She was giving in to his beguiling sorcery without a fight, and the knowledge of her physical vulnerability only sharpened her emotional resistance. With a frustrated mutter she jerked her head to one side, and pushed against his chest with all her might. James, surprised by the suddenness of her resistance, let her go. His bewildered gaze followed her movements as she stormed to the other side of the room.

Plopping into one of the two armchairs facing the desk, Caroline glanced over her shoulder and gestured toward his desk chair. "As I started to tell you before your hormones took over, I'm here on business. Now, shall we get on with this interview, or would you just prefer me to leave?"

Abruptly the confusion left his expression, to be replaced by indignation. "Do you mean you're the woman from Avery Temps I've been expecting?"

She nodded with a calm complaisance she only wished she could feel. Her heart sank when she noticed the brooding darkness that had entered his eyes.

"You really had no intention of ever seeing me again," he remarked tightly.

It wasn't really a question, but Caroline decided to treat it as such. "No," she murmured gently.

James flinched as though he'd been struck, and immediately a cold, hard mask settled over his features. The metamorphosis was so marked that Caroline could only stare at him in disbelief, unable to comprehend that this was the same man who had held her in his arms only moments before. Gone was the ardent lover, and in his place stood a tough, implacable individual whose features held a hard edge of cynicism.

In several long, controlled strides he had crossed the room and seated himself before her. The desk between them seemed as impenetrable as a mountain. Although James appeared relaxed as he leaned back against the charcoal padding of his swivel chair, his body held a formidable tension that seemed almost palpable. He reminded Caroline of a sleek black panther, waiting to unleash his energy on an unwary victim.

But she *was* prepared, she assured herself staunchly, and she had no intention of letting herself become a victim. The old Caroline had let herself be cowed and intimidated, and she had been manipulated in the name of love. But that woman was a shadow from her past and had no place in her future. The new Caroline was fashioned of sterner stuff; she had to be, if she wanted to maintain her self-respect. You're strong enough to stand on your own, she reminded herself silently, clasping her hands in her lap.

Then she met James's gaze across the distance that separated them, and fear became an acrid taste in her mouth. His eyes were burning a message of possession into her brain, making her aware of how badly she yearned to draw on his strength. The night they had met, she'd needed succor from the storm and shelter from the pain of Frank's defection. James had given her both, and she had never been able to forget the warm delight of that giving.

But in the intervening months she had changed, and no longer needed a safety net to catch her if she fell. She could deal alone with the blows life inflicted on her, but to do so she had to strengthen her confidence in herself. She could no longer afford the luxury of leaning on anyone else, and she had to remember that. Emotional dependence was a trap guaranteed to strip her of her individuality, and she never again wanted to be fettered by those silken bonds. Dear Lord, she had to remember that!

Caroline noticed the intent way James was gazing at her lips. There was both hunger and longing in his eyes, but there was also a degree of masculine assurance that rubbed her the wrong way. Immediately she tilted her chin in a mute gesture of defiance, and the sensuality that had begun to soften the curve of his mouth was erased in an instant. "What are your qualifications?" he asked impatiently.

She wanted to snap back at him, but resisted the temptation. After all, his current attitude was largely her fault. He couldn't be blamed for having drawn his own conclusions as to why she'd suddenly reappeared in his life, she thought nervously, especially when she considered how single-minded he'd been in trying to find her. After all the time and money he must have spent in his search, the least she could do was offer him the courtesy due a prospective employer.

"I've just completed a basic six-month business course, which has mainly concentrated on secretarial and computer skills."

"Full-time?"

"Evenings," she muttered defensively. "I've had to work days."

He grabbed a pencil from the top of his desk, and began to tap annoyingly on the legal pad in front of him. His eyes narrowed, his voice was a sarcastic drawl as he asked, "Isn't your ex paying you alimony and child support?"

James had hit a sore spot. Since they'd separated, Frank had been less than regular in his support payments, and although it was already June she was still waiting for May's check. He had made every excuse in the book for his inability to fulfill his obligations to Pete and herself, but he had never once hinted at what she suspected was the truth. According to the gossip of a few well-meaning friends, Frank was trying to hold on to his young love by living in the fast lane. Although she had no firsthand experience of that, Caroline assumed that life in the fast lane was expensive.

Yet she allowed none of the worry or anger caused by her thoughts to surface, and managed to fix a smile on her face as false as the one James was wearing. "Of course," she finally managed to reply. "But I try to put as much as possible into the college fund Frank and I started for Pete a few years ago."

Prepared as she was for some kind of derisive rejoinder, her surprise was all the greater when James commented quietly, "You're quite a woman, and Peter is lucky he's got you for a mother, Caroline. I think I've told you that before."

Flushing with pleasure at the unexpected praise, she grimaced and shrugged her shoulders. "Not that I've managed to up the principal a great deal. I never realized how many hidden expenses would pop up in the last year. Pete took a job working weekends and after school to help out, but there never seemed to be enough money. Studio pictures, his graduation trip, the senior ball. That last nearly had me tearing my hair out by the roots!''

He didn't respond to her laughter by so much as a smile. Instead his eyes darkened, and his features hardened with quick anger. ''Damn it, there was no need for you to make those kind of sacrifices!''

''There was every need,'' she remarked stiltedly. ''There were bills to pay, food to buy, and security to provide for my son. It's bad enough that he has a father who—''

Although Caroline bit back the rest of her words, it wasn't in time to prevent James from probing into what she'd left unsaid. ''He has a father who...what, Caroline?''

She lowered her head, but not before she'd exposed the sheen of tears in her eyes to his discerning gaze. ''One who ignores him as though he no longer exists.''

''I knew by the way he treated you that he was callous, but what the hell kind of man would cut his own son out of his life?''

''A man who's trying to pretend the years haven't caught up with him,'' she replied tiredly. ''One who is head over heels in love with a girl barely two years older than his son.'' She looked up and gave a laugh devoid of humor. ''Pete is taller than his father, has black hair and blue eyes, and is what the girls commonly refer to as a hunk. Need I go on?''

"The poor kid," James muttered huskily.

Although she'd managed to control her tears, Caroline couldn't control the sadness in her voice. "He tries to hide his pain, but I've watched it change him, James. He's had to grow up faster than I wanted him to."

His eyes glinted with sympathy. "It had to happen sooner or later."

"I know, but he's become overly protective of me in the process." She shook her head and allowed the worry that had been eating at her for months to surface. "He's talking about getting a job full-time instead of attending college and that scares me to death. Ever since I can remember, Pete's wanted to train as a lawyer and later enter the political arena. He's bright and energetic enough to fulfill his goals if he's given the chance. I thought when he won a partial sports scholarship it would reinforce my arguments, but he just changes the subject whenever I mention college."

"He's old enough to make his own decisions."

"But not if it means having to compromise his dreams and ambitions for my comfort and security," she responded fiercely. "I won't have him sacrifice his future for me."

Acknowledging that Caroline had been sent by Avery Temps had been quite a blow to James's ego, but it was nothing he couldn't handle. As he saw it, the real problem was Caroline's attitude toward him, which was defensive at best and downright hostile at worst. He knew she had more reason than most to distrust men, but she had to accept that he wasn't cut from the same cloth as her husband. He was fully aware that she was like no woman he'd ever known before.

It wasn't just a sexual attraction he felt for Caroline; he had been around the block enough times to be certain of that. Even before they'd made love she'd managed to tap his gentler emotions, bringing to the fore a protective side to his personality that he'd never suspected existed. She was no longer the lost, vulnerable waif of the storm, yet his desire to take on the burden of her pain and hardship was as strong as ever.

Caroline was . . . special. Certainly no other woman could have managed to turn his life inside out with so little effort, he thought with a tart edge of amusement. He hadn't been exaggerating when he told her he'd nearly gone crazy looking for her. Of course, his staff hadn't been amused by his surly temper. Within a month of meeting Caroline, his private secretary of two years had quit her job and moved on to greener, more salubrious pastures. Even his friends had begun to step lightly around him.

The next two people he had hired hadn't lasted through their training period, which was why he'd been forced to take on a succession of temporary help. The women from Avery Temps hadn't lasted long, either, but since they weren't supposed to it wasn't as embarrassing when they left. He frowned, and scratched an indentation in the pencil he held with his thumbnail. He didn't want to hire Caroline. Things were difficult enough without placing himself in a position of authority over her, yet he wasn't about to let her walk away from him. They belonged together, though she still needed to be convinced of that.

Slowly James began to roll the pencil between his fingers, staring down at it as though it held some kind of fascination.

For Caroline, the silence between them was becoming uncomfortable, and she edgily shifted her weight. His face was expressionless, which made her even more nervous. In the last half hour she had come to realize that James was at his most dangerous to her peace of mind when he displayed his stone face, and she wondered what thoughts had triggered this concentration.

It wasn't long before her curiosity was satisfied. With a final twirl James dropped the pencil onto the green blotter covering his desk, and rested his chin on his steepled fingers. "Does Pete resent the men you date?"

Whatever she'd expected, it hadn't been this. Caroline stared at him in some bewilderment. "I...I haven't gotten around to dating, so the question hasn't arisen."

A momentary satisfaction entered his eyes but was quickly blocked from her view by the descent of his eyelids. "Then how do you think he'll react to another man in your life?"

"There is no other man," she insisted in goaded tones. "If there were, I think Peter would be happy for me."

"Then there's the solution to your problem," he said quietly, his lashes abruptly lifting to reveal the full intensity of his gaze. "Marry me, and your son will no longer have to worry about your welfare. For that matter, you won't have to worry about his. I'm well endowed with my fair share of this world's goods, with no one to spend them on. If his grades are up to par, I'll send Peter to Harvard and later sponsor his political career."

She sat up straight, her spine so tense that she feared it might crack. "What . . . what did you say?"

"Let me be that other man in your life, darlin'."

Seven

Caroline rose to her feet with a measure of dignity, but the pain she was feeling glittered in her eyes as she looked down at James. She had expected more from him, not least to be taken seriously. Right now all she wanted to do was sit down on his plush carpet and howl with disappointment. But that was the kind of sniveling, weak behavior he expected from her, she thought, with a cynical appraisal that tore at her pride.

Wrapping her disappointment and indignation around her like a cloak, she asked, "Did you really think I'd accept your bribe, James?"

He had been sitting with wary alertness, but the bitterness in her voice galvanized him into action. Within seconds his hands were gripping the softly rounded flesh of her upper arms through her silk blouse, his expression remorseful as he studied her pale features. "Caroline, you don't understand."

"What don't I understand? That you want me badly enough to pay a very high price for the privilege? Believe me, you've just made that more than clear."

"I'm not ashamed of wanting you." He ground out the words harshly, his eyes blazing golden fire. "You're reacting as though I'd made you an indecent proposition. Would you rather consider the role of mistress?"

"As a matter of fact I would," she muttered with overt sarcasm. "At least then I wouldn't feel you owned me lock, stock and barrel."

"There would be no need for you to feel that way," he protested. "I'd provide you with a generous allowance, and you would have more freedom of choice in your life than you do now, Caroline."

The man certainly believed in digging a deep grave, she thought incredulously. Couldn't he see how insulting he was being, or was he totally blind to anyone's needs but his own? She uttered a sharp, disparaging laugh. "Wouldn't you do the same for a mistress?"

His eyes narrowed dangerously. "Are you really lobbying for the position?"

Caroline's mouth was suddenly dry, and she swallowed hastily. "No." Her denial wasn't as forceful as she would have wished, but fortunately James missed the slight quiver in her voice. Clearing her throat, she added, "I'm sorry if I gave you the wrong impression."

"What you're giving me is a headache."

She glowered at him mutinously. "Just because I turned down an offer to become your mistress?"

"I'm offering you marriage, damn it!"

"Why?"

Visibly taken aback by the abruptness of her question, he hesitated. When he finally spoke, his voice held the softness of velvet.

She shivered as the sensual drawl rippled over her flesh like a caressing hand. "Because I want to have the right to take care of you, Caroline."

"I can take care of myself."

"But you're a gentle, sensitive soul, and you shouldn't have to work yourself to a standstill just to make ends meet. You're so special. When we made love I felt a wholeness, a kind of completion I'd never experienced before with any other woman. You gave yourself to me with such a sweet generosity of spirit that I was touched in ways that shocked and delighted me. When I woke up in that bed alone, it was as if a part of me had been cut away. I knew then that you belonged to me and always would. I need you in my life."

It was entirely the wrong explanation to give, and Caroline's mouth curved scornfully as she exploded in anger. "*You* want, *you* need! Well, what about what I want and need for myself? I am a competent human being with my own goals and ambitions, but that doesn't matter to you as long as you get your own way. You offer me your name, your worldly goods, your broad shoulders to lean on, as though I'm incapable of surviving on my own merits. The one thing you didn't offer me was respect, and in my eyes it's the only thing worth having, James.''

His fingers tightened, biting into her flesh with a growing pressure. ''I wouldn't want to marry a woman I didn't respect.''

''Then why try to bribe me?'' she responded.

''I didn't . . . God give me patience!'' Releasing her with an abruptness that left her off balance, he placed several feet of space between them. ''All right, maybe I should have voiced my intentions with more delicacy, but you don't inspire a man with a hell of a lot of confidence.''

Clutching the back of her chair for support, she snapped, ''Do you think my self-esteem was improved by being told that you'll take care of me? In a pig's eye, Mr. Mitchel!''

James fixed her with a steely glare. ''What in the devil is wrong with a man wanting to take care of the woman he loves?''

Caroline's anger was diffused in a heartbeat, and in its place was a tenderness she didn't want to feel. Damn him, he was getting to her . . . really getting to her! James looked so much like a belligerent boy, his chin tilted pugnaciously, his cheeks mottled with an angry flush. But the expression in his eyes was far from childlike, and guilt tore through her like summer lightning. It wasn't right to salvage her pride at the expense of his own, especially when she'd learned the hard way that pride and self-respect go hand in hand.

Desperately Caroline glanced around her, understanding how an animal must feel when cornered. The trap had been sprung and she could visualize a cage looming in the distance, a luxurious one to be sure, but still a cage. Eventually as if drawn by a magnet, her gaze returned to James and she drew in a sharp, uneven breath as she acknowledged the attractiveness of the bait. He had moved to stand by the window, his back to her as he stared into the distance.

He had isolated himself in an aura of indifference, but she could see the truth and it struck an answering spark inside her. James was lonely. He was a man who had forged chains of power and influence that set him apart from most people. Somehow she had managed to slip underneath his usual guard, and had touched a heart as wary of trust as her own. Her throat constricted until swallowing was painful, and she shivered as the cold wind of reason blew through her mind.

She ached to go to him, to press herself against the rigid back and comfort him with her presence. She wanted to touch hearts and bodies and souls, until neither of them need ever be lonely again. She wanted to crawl inside his embrace and bask in the warm security of his affection, but the very intensity of her emotions toward him made that impossible. She was too uncertain of who she was to give him what he needed from her.... That was the bottom line.

James deserved a competent woman who was certain of her own strengths, not one who constantly doubted herself. They had met too soon for her to have discovered what she was capable of achieving on her own, and if she married him, those questions would never be answered. She was too afraid of losing herself to another man; of subduing her own personality within what he expected of her. No, she couldn't afford to love a man like James Mitchel.

Her thoughts reminded her of the words he'd spoken such a short time ago, and she whispered, "You don't love me, James. You love the image of me you've built in your mind, but that's not the real woman!"

Slowly he turned and started toward her. "I know the difference between fantasy and reality. I've known it from the moment we met, but I can see that I'm going to have to convince you."

The melting heat in his steady gaze was having that unfortunate effect on her knees again, but she stood her ground. "How...?" She cleared her throat nervously and began again. "How do you propose to do that?"

He winced and grimaced ruefully. "Did you have to use that particular term?"

Caroline would have stamped her foot in frustration, if she'd thought her knee would hold up under the strain. Instead she darted a swift, suspicious glance upward and carefully rephrased her question. "What are you up to?"

"I suggest a compromise."

She didn't trust that innocent tone in his voice, any more than she trusted the devilish glint in his wide brown eyes. "What kind of a compromise?" she asked guardedly.

"You come to work here for a trial period of say..." He paused while he settled himself on a corner of the desk, and studied his polished snakeskin boot tip with complete absorption. "One month. That should do it."

Caroline wished she had a purse to bash him over the head with. "Do what?"

"Give you the time you need to get to know me a little better."

"What are you getting out of this so-called compromise?"

He gestured toward the pile of papers and letters overflowing the metal In tray on his desk. "I get a secretary to help me with this mess, as well as someone who can keep me in line if my masculine ego threatens to get out of control." He uttered a rueful laugh. "You may have to be trained to do the former, but you have to admit that you're already overqualified at handling my ego."

"And when the trial period is over?"

He slapped his palms against his thighs and pushed himself swiftly to his feet. "We reevaluate."

Caroline started nervously, but she did manage not to cringe when he held out his hand to her.

"Is it a deal?" he asked silkily.

Pausing long enough to question her sanity, she slipped her fingers into his grasp. "It's a deal!"

Caroline was hunched over her kitchen table, her eyelids drooping as she stared down at the empty bowl in front of her. Her son was seated across from her, eating his dinner and apparently unaware that his mother was dying. Listlessly she looked in his direction, and a fond smile replaced the droop that had earlier distorted her mouth. It wasn't Peter's fault she was dying; it was the fault of that wolf in sheep's clothing.

Even with Linda's prior warning to cushion the shock, she hadn't been prepared for the reality of working for James. It was true he pushed himself harder than anyone else on his staff, but the man was a human dynamo. He had a clear, incisive mind that operated with computer precision, and didn't seem to realize that not everyone had his reserves of energy. She certainly didn't, she thought glumly, toying with the latticed edge of her place mat.

When she paused to look back over the past couple of weeks, she wondered how she'd avoided a nervous breakdown. She supposed pure, stiff-necked pride had proven to be her salvation. It was the only explanation she could come up with that made any sense. From day one James had pushed her relentlessly, teaching her things both related to his office and to the operation of the newspaper in general. She had pushed back just as hard, determined to prove herself capable of handling her job.

It was only after the first grueling week was almost over that she made a discovery that completely altered the way she thought about James as a boss. She was standing at the sink in the lunchroom, swallowing two aspirin while mentally trying to prepare herself to return to her desk. James had come up behind her and placed a hand on her shoulder in a comforting gesture.

"Bad headache?" he murmured dryly. "It's no wonder, with the pressure I've been putting on you."

She shrugged away from his touch and threw the empty paper cup into a nearby wastebasket. "I'm coping."

"You're more than coping," he surprised her by saying. "I've been meaning to tell you what a great job you're doing, but every time I turn around there seems to be another crisis to distract me."

She looked at him, an incredulous expression on her face. His eyes held sincere approval, and she absorbed his compliment with a rush of pleasure. She had been certain that he'd thrown her in at the deep end just to see her drown, but she should have known that James had too much integrity to win by a foul. He was honest and straightforward in his dealings with people, both professionally and personally. She'd seen constant evidence of it since she'd started working for him, but had been too blind to admit to the truth.

She felt her resentment melting away, and for the first time noticed the lines of fatigue pulling at the corners of his mouth. Before she could stop herself, she exclaimed, "You look exhausted."

James nodded and leaned his head against the wall, his large body uncharacteristically still. He lowered his lashes, and Caroline saw how the dark fringe blended with the shadows beneath his eyes. "I haven't been sleeping worth a damn."

"Worrying about the drop in circulation?" she inquired sympathetically.

"About that and other things," he replied with a dispirited sigh. "I got a call from Manny Ruiz's wife last night."

Emanuel Ruiz, affectionately referred to as Manny the Man, was a great favorite among the staff. A bluff, hearty individual, he had a booming laugh that filled a room like warm sunshine and a smile for everyone he encountered as he went about his duties as custodian. She'd heard it said that he'd been with the *Sacramento News* from the day it had first opened and there was no doubt about the concern she could see deepening the lines on James's face.

"What's wrong?" she questioned, for the first time realizing she hadn't seen The Man yesterday. "Has something happened to Manny?"

The cords in James's neck tightened. "He forgot how to get to work."

"He forgot...." She grew still, a sensation of dread creeping over her. "What do you mean?"

His eyes opened slowly, and he fixed her with a gentle glance. "Didn't you know he's suffering from Alzheimer's disease, Caroline?"

She shook her head and whispered huskily, "No, how could I?"

"It's not common knowledge, but you know how quickly gossip spreads in this place. I was afraid..." He paused. "Manny was too ashamed to have anyone know about his illness."

"Ashamed!"

"He's a man," he exclaimed harshly. "What in the hell is he supposed to feel, when he knows what he's going to become?"

"It's not his fault."

James slammed his clenched fist against the edge of the sink and turned his face away from her startled scrutiny. "Don't you think I know that? He's been one of my people for over fifteen years and I care about him, Caroline. He's a good man, the best, and this kind of thing shouldn't happen to someone like Manny. When I've been down he's always been there with a laugh or a joke, but he can't remember the jokes anymore."

He broke off what he was saying and drew in a shaken breath. When he continued, his voice held a haunted note of horror. "The doctors informed Luisa that the disease is progressing faster than they'd anticipated. In a matter of months The Man won't recognize anyone, even himself in a mirror. He won't remember how to laugh or to cry or—''

Giving a distressed cry, Caroline gripped his forearm. "Stop it, James! Don't do this to yourself."

"I'm sorry," he muttered gruffly. "I just feel so damned helpless."

Although his features appeared hard, even implacable, there was a suspicious hint of moisture shining in his eyes. Caroline spread her fingers against his forearm and began to rub the bunched muscles soothingly. "There's nothing you can do but continue to provide emotional support to his family. How is his wife holding up under the strain?"

"Luisa has the strength of a saint and the serenity of an angel, but she's been worrying about finances. The doctors have warned her that eventually Manny will need more care than she can provide at home, and their insurance won't cover more than a few months in a convalescent hospital. I assured her that the paper will incur any expenses on Manny's behalf, but she balked at the idea of charity." A faint smile curved his mouth. "She's as full of stubborn pride as you are, Caroline. It took me the devil's own time to convince her that it wasn't charity being offered, but a reward for Manny's faithful years of service."

Caroline's heart went out to the other woman, and she asked worriedly, "Manny's not old enough to draw social security, is he? Will Luisa be able to manage on his pension?"

"Although he's a couple of years short of qualifying for full retirement, I'll see that he gets it!"

There was only one way James could guarantee the Ruizes' full retirement benefits, she realized, and that was by subsidizing them himself. She also knew that there was no extended convalescent coverage on the group insurance policy that covered the *Sacramento News* employees. Since he was the paper's owner, James had just accepted responsibility for what could amount to years of very expensive treatment.

It was then that Caroline absorbed the full extent of the commitment James had made to the people who worked for him. He loved them like the family he didn't have. That was why he could bark orders like an army general, snarl, snap, roar his head off like the lion they called him, and still have the respect and devotion of every member of his staff. Because when the chips were down, they all knew he'd be there for them, just as he was for Manny and Luisa. Just as he'd been for her!

From that day on Caroline hadn't minded the long hours or the amount of stress that was part and parcel of being James Mitchel's assistant. With a smile she traced the embossed leaf pattern on her coffee cup with a languid finger. She typed and filed, answered phones and learned to do pasteup ads. She fetched and carried with the best of them. She went about her tasks with eager willingness, gaining a quiet sense of satisfaction from knowing that she eased some of the tremendous work load James carried.

A wide yawn took her by surprise, and she stretched her arms over her head to ease the tight knot that had formed in her shoulders. "Aren't you through eating yet?" she asked Pete, giving him a blinky-eyed stare. "I want to do the dishes and get to bed."

"They're already done," he replied cheerfully, "except for that soup bowl you've been dozing into for the past twenty minutes."

She blinked again and noticed the cleared table and stove top. "Oh, honey, thank you."

"You sure spend a lot of time in Lala Land since you've gone to work for the paper." He whirled a kitchen chair and straddled it, resting his crossed arms across the back as he gazed at her impishly. "Even when you're here, you're not really here...if you catch my drift."

She gave him a guilty look. "Oh, Pete! I haven't spent very much time with you lately, have I?"

He raised an admonishing hand in the air. "Hey, I'm not complaining. With both of us working full-time and my extra hours at work on the weekends, we haven't had much chance for togetherness."

She plopped an elbow onto the table and rested her chin on her fist. "You're working too hard."

"Nah, I have plenty of time to carouse."

"I wish I had your energy," she complained in slightly peeved accents. "Maybe then I'd be a better mother. Grilled cheese sandwiches...yuck!"

Her disgusted grimace caused him to grin widely. "I'm a big boy now, Mom. Just ask Pammy, if you don't believe me."

Pamela Farr was the girl he'd been dating for the past couple of months, a gorgeous blonde with a knockout figure and a suggestive giggle that irritated the pudding out of Caroline. At the mention of her name, Caroline scowled darkly. "You just watch your step, Mr. Big Britches. I'm too young to become a grandmother."

With a rakish tilt of one black eyebrow, he drawled outrageously, "It isn't my step I need to watch."

Pursing her lips, she blew an errant strand of hair out of her eyes. "Peter, how long has it been since I've sent you to bed without your dinner?"

This time both of his eyebrows rose in an expression of mock innocence. "You're too late, I've already eaten."

Caroline subdued the smile that threatened, her eyes sparkling as she delighted in her son's company. "You call grilled cheese sandwiches and chicken noodle soup dinner?"

"It was a gourmet feast, a delight to the senses, a delicious..."

Giggling uncontrollably, she lifted both hands in a gesture of surrender. "All right, you've convinced me I haven't failed in the mother department."

His smile faded abruptly. "You aren't the one who's a failure as a parent."

"Pete, I..." She swallowed to ease the lump that had formed in her throat and fixed him with a pleading gaze. "You have a right to be bitter, but you can't let your father's selfishness ruin your life."

He avoided her eyes by staring down at the table. "I called his office today."

Caroline's muscles clenched in mute protest, but she managed to appear unruffled as she asked, "Why did you phone him, Pete?"

"To tear a strip off him for not sending his support payments the last two months."

"How do you know he hasn't...?"

Her question dwindled into thin air as she looked into his eyes and caught her breath on a gasp. It was a man who looked back at her, one with anger to sustain the strength of his convictions and the maturity to control that anger. "You've been checking the mail," she concluded flatly. "I'm sorry I tried to keep you in the dark, but I didn't want to worry you, Peter. You've been disillusioned enough, and there's already too much antagonism between you and your father."

"So you expect me to just sit back and do nothing, while you kill yourself working overtime to make up the difference?"

"You know I love my job."

"That's not the point." He stood suddenly and clutched the back of his chair with such force that his knuckles whitened. "Dad should face up to his responsibilities, but that tramp he's shacked up with has him spinning in circles. You know, in a way I almost feel sorry for the poor creep. From some of the gossip I've heard, he's having a tough time keeping his little girlfriend happy."

"That's none of our business, Peter."

His lip curled with a cynicism that belied his youth. "It is when you're the one to suffer for his blasted fling, Mother."

"Have you heard me complaining?" she asked stiffly.

"Of course not, although dear old Dad seems to think differently."

Caroline drew in a sharp breath, but managed to keep the anger out of her voice. "I'm not interested in what Frank thinks...not anymore."

"That's pretty much what I said, before I aired a few opinions of my own." He gave a dry, unamused laugh and stared at the wall behind her. "I told him he was a poor father and a worse husband, and that as far as I was concerned he wasn't much of a man. I also let him know he could go straight to hell and stay there for all I cared."

Caroline closed her eyes, anguished by the underlying pain in her son's voice. She remembered how often in the past Peter had sought his father's approval and been disappointed. Why hadn't Frank ever taken the time to get to know his child, to value the love he'd been offered? He had taken Pete for granted, and now she was afraid that the wall of resentment between them was too high ever to be scaled.

She studied the strained features before her with compassion. She didn't know what to say to ease Peter's bitter disillusion, so didn't even try. Instead she decided to appeal to his sense of practicality. "You know you didn't mean that, honey. He's your father and you love him."

"And he only loves himself," her son retorted harshly. "If he needs his little whore to stroke his manly ego so badly, then let him have her. I've made plans of my own, and they don't include depending on him any longer than absolutely necessary!"

Caroline's body grew stiff at the ambiguousness of his statement, and she felt the blood seep slowly from her face. "What kind of plans, Peter?"

"I've been thinking about joining the Air Force." His chest expanded as he drew in a breath, but his gaze didn't falter. "They offer all kinds of career opportunities, and since I'd be getting room and board, I'd be able to send you money every month."

Caroline felt completely defeated as she searched her son's determined features, and only the knowledge of how much she knew he wanted to complete his education gave her the strength to argue. "Peter, I can support myself without any assistance from you or your father. Forgoing college now would only create more problems later. You should be worrying about your future and not your mother."

"You're not being practical," he countered stubbornly. "We can't afford it, Mom."

"I'll sell the house."

"You wouldn't have much left over," he interrupted sharply. "Not once you'd paid off the second mortgage Dad took out a few years ago to finance that stupid get-rich-quick scheme of his."

Caroline had hoped he'd never gotten wind of the shaky real estate deal Frank and a few of his friends had put together, but she should have known that a boy of nearly fifteen would have figured out what was going on. Heaven knows, Pete had heard them arguing often enough. She'd been against taking such a financial risk, but as usual Frank had persuaded her to go along with him. When the deal went belly-up, she'd been resigned to the loss, yet now she could have wrung her own neck for being such a gullible fool!

But crying over past mistakes wasn't going to get her anywhere, and with an encouraging smile she said, "Look, sweetheart, you've already earned a partial scholarship and I don't object to you working part-time as long as it doesn't interfere with your grades. If we budget carefully, I'm sure there'll be enough in the savings to take up the slack."

His mouth firmed with familiar obstinacy. "You'd be left with nothing to fall back on."

"I'm only thirty-seven, for heaven's sake, and certainly healthy enough to go on working for the things that matter to me. Your future is my main concern. Can't you see that?"

Caroline's anxious insistence finally pierced her son's opposition, and an exasperated Pete ran a hand through his dark hair. Ruefully grinning at her, he said, "You know, I think I inherited my stubbornness from you."

Caroline felt faint with relief at having gained a reprieve, however momentary. "You know," she repeated with a smile of her own, "I believe you did."

Eight

"Caroline I'd like to see you in my office before you leave."

The sigh Caroline gave as she looked up at James was one half resigned and one half annoyed. Returning her purse to the bottom drawer of her desk, she slid the metal panel closed with more force than subtlety. Just once, she fumed as she obediently rose to her feet, she'd like to leave work at a reasonable hour. Just once she'd like to hear the maddening man say please. Just once she'd like to hear herself say no. With a whole list of "justs" rattling around in her brain, she reluctantly followed James into his office.

He closed the door and motioned toward a chair. She sat down, and he added to her discomposure by perching himself on the desk directly in front of her. Keeping a reasonable amount of distance between them had become something of a game to Caroline, but one that was necessary if she wanted to remain in full control of herself. Whenever James stepped over the invisible barriers, her body seemed to react with a will of its own.

As it was doing now, she was to discover, dismayed. Her heart was pumping madly, sweat from the palms of her hands was making the wooden arms of her chair sticky, and her mouth had gone completely dry. She flexed her fingers and tried to concentrate on regulating her breathing, but the sizzling sparks arching between James and herself weren't making it easy.

Caroline lowered her head and wriggled nervously. Crossing her denim-clad legs, she noticed with objective appreciation, her thighs no longer bulged. And she experienced a pleasant surge of satisfaction. Glad to have a distraction, she blocked out her awareness of James's body by concentrating on her own. Divorce and entering the work force had had a salutary effect on her figure, she decided with a twinge of amusement, and she no longer had to worry about buying pants with expando waists.

But her attempted diversion failed when she found herself wondering if James had noticed the pounds she'd shed, and if he liked her new slenderness. A vivid image shot to the forefront of her mind, and she saw again the masculine appreciation in his slumbrous gaze as his hands caressed her body. He certainly hadn't been put off by her ample figure that night, she remembered with a shiver of response. In fact, he'd been especially pleased by the fullness of her breasts.

Caroline swallowed heavily, praying that the dark eyes that were casually inspecting her cotton blouse wouldn't notice her hardened nipples trying to poke through the rumpled material. His arms were crossed across his chest in what she now recognized as a habitual pose. This close he was all intimidating, overpowering male, and she felt her trembling increase alarmingly.

Nervously she looked away from the muscular spread of his thighs, and leaned as far back from him as she could without toppling over in her chair. She wondered why, since it was *his* stone-washed jeans that were so tight, she was the one with the breathing difficulties. She also wondered why her gaze kept wandering back to forbidden territory. And James was forbidden to her. She'd have to remember that.

James's eyes gleamed with awareness of her discomfort, but all he said was, "You've been here a month, Caroline."

She gasped, her hands clenching as she realized why he wanted to talk to her. "I'd forgotten all about our trial period," she said faintly. "The time's passed very quickly."

With a grunt of acknowledgment he shifted his weight to one hip, and her eyes followed his foot as it began swinging back and forth. It was a relaxed movement, one which oddly increased her own tension. She clasped her hands over her knees and felt them quivering weakly. He still had a most peculiar effect on her knees, not to mention what his closeness did to the rest of her body.

James saw a dimple flash against the corner of her mouth, and desperately wanted to dip his tongue into that tiny crevice. But he stopped himself before he could follow up on the thought, reminded of the patient restraint he'd exercised around Caroline since he'd hired her. Patience, that was a good word. Caroline needed his patience. He'd have to remember that.

Don't blow it now, Mitchel, he mentally warned himself before he could lunge at her. You're almost at the home stretch. He tried not to fantasize about what he'd do when he got there. It had been difficult enough keeping his hands off Caroline this past few weeks, without allowing his imagination to go haywire. Clearing his throat, he asked thickly, "You've been happy here?"

Her face flushed with delicate color. "You know I have, James. The work is interesting and constantly challenging, but that isn't what pleases me most. There's a certain atmosphere among the staff, a comradery I didn't find anywhere else I worked. This place is so full of life and movement and . . ." She paused to regain control of her tripping tongue, and waved her hand enthusiastically in the air. "Everyone's been so friendly and helpful, I feel like I belong."

"You do belong, Caroline. That's what I asked you in here to discuss." He studied her vibrant features with tender thoroughness before saying quietly, "I called Linda Avery today and sang your praises. Although she responded with gracious diplomacy, I think she was feeling pretty smug because you'd managed to go the distance."

Caroline gave him a mocking look through demurely lowered lashes. "Linda was afraid she was throwing me to the wolves, but I convinced her I could soothe the savage beast with one hand tied behind my back."

Although James's eyes sparkled dangerously, he let the taunt pass. "She cares a great deal for you."

"Yes," Caroline murmured softly. "Linda's a good friend and an even stauncher supporter. Between her encouragement and Peter's, I haven't been given a chance to worry about failing."

"You had nothing to worry about," he responded gruffly, returning his attention to the shine on his boots. "As I told Ms. Avery, you're a conscientious and intelligent employee, and I let her know that as far as I'm concerned your position on the staff of *Sacramento News* is permanent. She said to tell you how happy she was for you, and that she'd call you in a few days and take you out for a celebratory lunch. That is, if there's anything to celebrate. Is there, Caroline? Does the idea of putting up with a beast like me for an indeterminate length of time put you off?"

Caroline wanted to jump up and throw her arms around James, but was so disconcerted by that mad, impulsive thought that she remained glued to her

chair. They had established a good working relationship, and the last thing she should do was throw a
wrench in the works by being overly affectionate.
James seemed to have gotten over his brief infatua-
tion with her, and that was the way she wanted things
to continue. Yes, she decided, ignoring the strange
sinking feeling in the pit of her stomach, she was perfectly satisfied with her life as it was.

Caroline thought she saw disappointment at her
lack of enthusiasm cloud James's eyes, and was certain of it when he repeated, "Does the idea of staying
here have any appeal, Caroline?"

She was pleased with his businesslike attitude toward her, she told herself firmly, disregarding the
niggling little jab of dissatisfaction she felt at his
sharpened tone. Needing to lighten the suddenly tense
atmosphere between them, she forced herself to form
a teasing smile. "Although my boss is a bit of a beast
at times, it's usually because he forgets to eat or holes
up in his office for too many hours at a stretch.
Generally speaking, he's a pretty nice guy, and I'm
beginning to think he can't do without me."

James felt his heart give a lurch and resume beating
with a furious rhythm. Caroline didn't realize how
right she was. In a short time she'd become indispens-
able to him, her bright mind and enthusiastic assistance causing him to wonder how he'd ever gotten
along without her. But in an understandable way, his
increasing dependence on her made him uneasy. All

the need seemed to be on his side, which didn't bode well for his chances of a future with her.

When he'd hired Caroline it had been with a master plan in mind. First they would get to know each other on a business footing, then as friends, and last but not least as lovers. By using the water-dripping-on-stone method of wearing down her resistance, eventually he'd get her to agree to marry him. Simple, hah! His deductions were concise, logical, and far too calculated for his own peace of mind.

He had achieved his first objective far more thoroughly than he'd counted on. Caroline had equaled and then surpassed his expectations of a secretary, seeming to have an intuitive ability to sense his wishes before he was aware of them himself. He was delighted by her grit and determination; finding himself torn between her dreams and his own was an added complication. He was pleased with her growing self-assurance, yet wary of the unforeseen pressure it was adding to their relationship.

Too often he had found himself watching her for signs of vulnerability. At times he had consciously willed her to ask more from him on a personal level, but he'd waited in vain. She spent her days in a routine she'd quickly become comfortable with, and he felt about as necessary to her as a piece of furniture. The caterpillar was changing into a butterfly before his very eyes, and the woman he'd first known was too enthralled with trying out her new wings to be aware that she was flying away from him.

But he knew it, and the knowledge was killing him by degrees. He was also very proud of her. Maybe more than anyone, he wanted her to succeed in becoming her own person. But not if it means losing her, a taunting inner voice chided. You're not that noble and self-sacrificing, Mitchel. No, he wasn't, and he had to constantly struggle with his own guilt as a result of his paradoxical feelings toward her.

The terrible truth was that although he respected Caroline's desire for self-reliance, he still wanted her to be dependent on him for her happiness. In a nutshell, he wanted her to need him. Since his father had died, he'd had no one to share himself with, no one to dream with. His brief and bitterly disappointing marriage had only caused him to withdraw deeper into his cloak of isolation, until the night he'd met Caroline and gotten an idea of what had been missing from his life.

Honesty, gentleness, caring, loyalty...those had been alien values he hadn't really believed existed in any one woman. But her warmth had miraculously melted the repressive chains he'd forged around himself, and her need of him had given him the key to unlock his own heart. Love for her had flowed out and enriched every aspect of his existence, but it had also made him damnably vulnerable.

Caroline had made it clear that she didn't share his sentiments, and he was, to put it bluntly, scared that she never would. But he was so tired of walking alone, of having no one of his own to turn to when the darkness threatened his soul. Was it so wrong to want her to belong to him?

"James, are you all right?"

His head jerked up at the concern in her voice, and one look at her face gave him the answer to his question. His love for Caroline had gone beyond right and wrong, its existence growing independently of his wishes. She might not love him, but the physical attraction that still existed between them was undeniable. No matter what the outcome, he knew in that moment that he had to continue his pursuit.

To fail to do so would be to deny that love a chance to flourish and become the thing of beauty he knew it could be. He had to convince her that loving him needn't mean a loss of self. She was a healthy, vibrant woman with a deep core of sensuality still largely untapped. If the only way he could accomplish his ambitions was to use sex as a lever, then so be it. He was tired of living in a state of limbo, of being denied everything he held dear. Even though he hated the idea of trying to manipulate her, he justified his decision by telling himself that she wasn't leaving him much choice.

Stilling the niggling voice of his conscience, he assumed what he hoped was a confident expression. "I'm fine, just a little preoccupied."

"Is it something I can help you with?"

He smiled at her earnest expression, resisting the urge to smooth away the frown pleating her brows.

"You should be able to, since you're the reason for my brown study."

"I am?" she questioned uncertainly. "I don't understand."

"I'm trying to decide where to take you for dinner." Anticipating a refusal he added hurriedly, "To celebrate."

Caroline's breath puffed out of her chest in a rush, and she relaxed against the back of her chair with a chagrined expression. "You had me worried there for a minute. I thought you had a serious problem."

"I am very serious, Caroline," he corrected gently. "I want very much to take you out tonight."

Immediately she tensed, wariness clouding her eyes. "I don't think that would be a good idea."

He managed to paste a smile onto his face through sheer willpower. "I don't see any difficulty."

"You're my employer, and I—"

"And I'm a man, isn't that it?"

"Of course not!"

"Yet Linda Avery has been, to all intents and purposes, your boss, and you agree to see her socially."

"That's different," she argued impatiently. "She's my friend."

His mouth twisted mockingly. "Did sharing a bed for one night forever preclude friendship, Caroline?"

She flinched as though from a blow. Her voice shook as she protested, "That isn't fair."

"Neither is being treated like a pariah," he retorted grimly.

"Oh, I don't, I mean I . . ."

She paused to gather her composure, which was more than a bit ragged about the edges. James was using words to back her into a corner, but she was honest enough to admit to being relieved by this abrupt about-face. Only a short time ago she'd been certain he'd stopped thinking of her as anything other than a competent secretary, and now he was letting her know in no uncertain terms how wrong she'd been. She should have remembered that he was a genius when it came to confusing issues.

But confusion aside, she had to be sensible. Folding her hands primly in her lap, she said, "It's just that I don't believe in mixing business with . . . uh, I mean . . ."

"With pleasure?" he drawled, his eyes suddenly filled with wickedly dancing lights. "Would sharing a meal with me be a pleasure, sweetheart?"

"There you go," she muttered crossly, spearing him with a fulminating glance. "I'm trying to have a sensible discussion, and you start mouthing endearments!"

"That isn't all I'd like to mouth." His dark eyes trailed across her arched throat and down into the open V of her blouse.

Caroline jumped to her feet, which proved to be an enormous tactical error. Before she could stomp off in high dudgeon, James clamped his hands around her waist and casually drew her stiffly resistant body between his splayed thighs. She remained perfectly still.

Twisting to protest his dominance was out of the question, since already his eyes were on a level with her breasts.

The same thought occurred to James, and he used the knowledge shamelessly. Giving a sigh gusty enough to warm her skin from throat to belly button, he murmured, "We know each other a lot better now than we did a month ago, don't you agree?"

Caroline shivered. Determined to maintain a proper distance, she braced her hands against his collarbones. Unfortunately, the twin ridges she found there absorbed her attention and her reply was absentmindedly vague. "I suppose so."

James shrugged his shoulders, and the tips of her fingers automatically contracted. She looked down at her hands, dismayed to find they'd strayed closer to the unbuttoned opening of his shirt.

"Then your argument is no longer worth a hill of beans."

Her eyes jerked to his face, which had assumed a rather smug expression. "I think I missed something somewhere along the line," she remarked in confusion. "What argument are we talking about?"

"Don't you remember the day I hired you, when you told me I only loved the image of the woman I'd built up in my mind?" he questioned softly. "You didn't think I knew you well enough to be certain of my feelings, but you were wrong, sweetheart. You are more woman than I ever dreamed of meeting."

Her green eyes were clouded with turbulence. "James, please don't..."

"Don't love you?" he whispered huskily. "You're asking the impossible."

"What do you expect from me?" she cried defensively. "I can't give you what you want, don't you understand? I'm sorry I'm not ready for that kind of commitment, but it's the truth."

"Someday you'll be ready," he stated calmly, "and I plan to be there when you are. Until then I'll be satisfied with friendship, although that doesn't mean I won't try to coax you back into my bed. I'm a man, with a man's wants and needs, and I admit that living like a monk doesn't sit well on my shoulders. Frustration is playing hell with my temperament, but I haven't been able to look at another woman since the night we were together."

At her surprised exclamation he laughed, but it was a laugh more disparaging than amused. "Does that shock you, love? It shouldn't, not really. What we had was a lot more meaningful than either of us expected, and I believe in fidelity as deeply as you do."

"But you have no commitment to me," she whispered. "You're free to be with other women."

"It's you I want like hell on fire, no one else." He gave her a grin filled with self-mockery, and shook his head as though bemused by the admission. "You know, I wasn't supposed to tell you all this. I had the perfect seduction planned, but suddenly I don't have the stomach for any more subterfuge, Caroline. I want to touch you and hold you and lose myself again in your sweet body, and I'm praying you feel the same way. Do you desire me, or am I just tilting at windmills?"

Caroline wanted to hide behind a lie, but found herself saying, "Yes, but I'm just not ready...."

He pressed a gently admonishing finger against her lips. "I won't rush you or do anything you're not ready for. Just give us a chance, that's all I ask. I'm not going to push for marriage, if that's what you're worried about."

"And if I decide I have nothing to give?" she asked hesitantly. "Will that alter your decision?"

"Alter my...?" His question was never completed, and as he stared at her in tension-fraught silence, a terrible bleakness stiffened his features. With a muttered oath he pushed her away from him and lunged to his feet. "You once accused me of trying to bribe you, but I thought you knew me better than that by now."

"James, I didn't mean—"

"You damn well did mean." Anger and hurt vied for supremacy in his eyes. "But you can relax. The job is yours if you still want it, Caroline. I've never had to buy a woman and I'm damned if I'm going to start now!"

James pushed past her, his mouth rigid with anguish and disillusion. Pressing her knuckles against her lips, Caroline watched him walk away while sickness rose in her throat like bile. What had she done?

she asked herself in an agony of remorse. He had told her he loved her, only to be repulsed in the cruelest possible way.

In a blinding flash of self-awareness, she realized that she was making another man pay the price for her ex-husband's perfidy. Frank deserved her scorn and antipathy, but not James. Sweet heaven, not a man who had never shown her anything but kindness. James...whose heart was as big as his body. James...whose compassion and understanding she'd taken for granted. James...whom she scorned because she was too afraid to let herself love again. Oh, God! What had she done?

With a muffled sob she tore across the carpet and skirted the desks in the outer office. Through the wall of glass that fronted the street, she saw him disappear around the side of the building. Tears blurred her vision, causing her to fumble with the automatic pressure lock on the door. Once it was released, her damp palms slid across the bar, and she used the full force of her body to push it open.

Then she stood in a desolate daze of misery, while James's car screeched out of the parking lot next door and onto the street. He never looked back; never heard her scream his name. He didn't see her suddenly straighten, or observe the look of grim determination on her face. Nor did he see her reenter the deserted office and reach for the phone.

"Pete, I've been asked out to dinner tonight," she said when her son answered. "I'll probably be in very

late, so don't worry if I'm not home by the time you
get off your shift.''

Replacing the phone in its cradle, Caroline re-
trieved her purse and hurried toward the exit. The
visible evidence of her emotional turmoil had dried on
her cheeks, but she was still crying inside. She wept in
shame, she wept for James, but most of all she wept
for a woman who was too much of an emotional cow-
ard ever to allow herself to love again.

Nine

Caroline stood beside her compact car and stared up at James's home. The lovely structure had a balconied deck across the front and two separate wings that spread out and then doubled toward the back. The low-riding sun appeared larger than life, resembling a child's big orange beach ball. Its radiance bathed the wide expanse of window glass with sparkling prisms of vermilion, violet and gold light. She smiled as puffy white marshmallow clouds floated across the reflective surface, adding a touch of whimsy to the whole.

When James had first brought her here she'd been too distraught to notice the full beauty of her surroundings. Even if she hadn't been so distracted, the darkness and the inclement weather would have served as deterrents. But now she was able to appreciate the purity of design that let the house so successfully blend with its natural environs, and she was lost in admiration.

She glanced around her to study the gentle slope of lawn that formed a grassy carpet to the river. She basked in the quiet solitude, then she sighed. The heavy odor of the heat-laden foliage and late-summer flowers permeated her lungs. She returned her attention to the house. Amid this natural splendor it stood proud and tall and indomitable. It reminded her of James.

With renewed incentive Caroline walked across the drive, thrusting the long strap of her purse over her right shoulder. Her nervousness accelerated, and she impatiently brushed her hair away from her face. The sweet brackish scent of the river floated to her nostrils. Her feet crunched against the gravel driveway, then her steps echoed as she ascended the few stairs heading onto the natural redwood deck. The sounds were a reminder of the emptiness she felt inside.

Before she had a chance to knock, the door was pulled open and a disgruntled face peered out at her. "What are you doing here, Caroline?"

"I... May I come in?" Self-consciously she fanned the air in front of her and gave a strained laugh. "It's hot out here."

Gesturing her inside, James closed the door and preceded her into the living room. Nothing had changed from the way she remembered it, and Caro-

line was instantly catapulted into the past. Her eyes
darted from side to side with shy familiarity before
returning to settle on James's stern visage. But the
words clamoring for release in her mind suddenly
seemed impossible to speak, and she wanted to scream
at herself for her verbal impotence.

Of all times for her to be struck mute it was now,
when it was so important for her to be able to ease the
pain she'd inflicted on this man with such brutal cal-
lousness. Maybe that was why her tongue seemed
stuck to the roof of her mouth, because what she had
to say mattered too much. There was a lump of emotion lodged in her throat, and she swallowed heavily
to ease its tightness, praying she could somehow find
the words to resolve the dilemma she'd created
through her lack of understanding.

Caroline was well aware that every individual had
choices to make and paths to follow that would affect
the outcome of their lives. She stared at James, and
knew that earlier tonight she'd taken a wrong turn. He
was responding to her with coolly clinical deliber-
ation. His stance was rigidly defensive. Whatever else
he'd made her feel during their acquaintance, she
thought, it had never been that of an outsider looking
in. Yet that was exactly what she was experiencing
now, a sense of isolation and distance that seemed in-
surmountable.

He appeared dour and unapproachable, a stranger
inhabiting a familiar form. Even his eyes were different, she noticed with shocked recognition. Their

depths were curiously lackluster, as though a vital force had been removed from them. They no longer sparkled and gleamed with wickedly dancing lights. She wanted the old James back.

"Are you going to stand there staring at me all night, or will you eventually get around to telling me why you've come?" James pointed toward the large, cream-and-green modular sofa she remembered better than any other item of furniture in the room. "Have a seat."

Swinging her bag off her shoulder, Caroline held it in a death grip in front of her as she complied with his request. Keeping her head lowered, she plopped the bulky leather tote onto her lap and fiddled with its broken clasp. "James, I'm sorry."

The words were torn from vocal cords constricted with misery, a poor, croaking parody of what she'd intended them to be. Trying again, she just managed to elevate her voice above a rasping whisper. "I'm so very sorry, and I only hope you can forgive me for the way I treated you."

"There's nothing to forgive." His response was tired, the accompanying shrug of his shoulders dismissive. "If it makes you feel any better to hear it, I owe you an apology, too."

"Why should you feel the need to apologize?" Caroline bit her lip and reddened with embarrassment. "You weren't the one who caused a scene."

"I made an idiot of myself, as usual."

She muttered, "You did not make an idiot of your-self. I was the one who behaved with the graciousness of an irascible billy goat!"

James smiled at the image and dryly observed, "At least you don't have horns."

Her lips quivered momentarily, only to be pressed primly together in disapproval. "No, just a big mouth and not enough sense to know when to keep it closed."

"You only said what you thought, and if I didn't want to hear it that's my problem. You can't blame yourself for your honesty, especially after I admitted to being less than straightforward with you from the beginning."

"But that's just it. I didn't really say what I was thinking," she protested anxiously. "I used anger as a defense, so I wouldn't be forced to speak my mind."

He gave her a frustrated look and rifled his already mussed hair with one hand. "Postmortems aren't necessary, Caroline. I pushed and you pushed back. It was a predictable and entirely understandable re-action. Unfortunately for both of us, I'm not at my best when I'm being rejected. Hell—" he laughed bit-terly "—I'm never at my best around you!"

Spinning on his heel, James crossed in front of Caroline and went to stand by the window. His gaze followed the winding ribbon of the American River as it flowed past his property, and he felt envious of the passengers in a bright red pleasure boat as they sped over the water. He wished he could escape and share their laughter, feel the sun burn away the coldness he felt inside. The solace he usually gained from his favorite view was missing, anger and hurt and an aching sadness distorting any peace he might have found.

The source of his emotional turmoil was just behind him. He could feel her, sense her with every cell in his body, as though they were connected by invisible wires. Her presence could be dismissed with a few choice, vindictive words, but he couldn't bring himself to make her leave. It was funny in a sick kind of way, but he'd rather be miserable with Caroline than happy with anyone else.

"James, won't you let me explain?"

The deep pile of the carpet muffled her approach, and every muscle in his body clenched as he felt the delicate, yet searing pressure of her hand against his back. He caught her scent on an indrawn breath. It was a light, airy fragrance that reminded him of freshly picked flowers from a dew-dampened field. His head reeled as he turned to face her. "What is that perfume you always wear?"

Her hand dropped to her side, and she looked at him with wide, questioning eyes. Her hesitant laugh held a startled note as she asked, "What?"

"That perfume," James repeated huskily. "What's it called?"

"White Shoulders," she said on a suspended breath. "Do you like it?"

"White Shoulders," he whispered. His eyes closed, his nostrils flaring, he ruefully admitted, "It drives me crazy. You don't know how many unnecessary trips

I've made past your desk, just so I could remember the way it felt."

Caroline was puzzled by the cryptic words. "I don't..."

His lashes lifted to reveal hungry, haunted eyes. "The woman who comes in to clean for me thought I was crazy when I asked her not to change my bedding for a few days. The smell of you was everywhere, lingering on the sheets long after you'd gone. I'd lie there at night and remember the way you felt in my arms, tortured by a loneliness that struck all the way through to my soul."

A sob erupted from her chest. Her neck bent like the stem of a wilting flower, and her forehead found the support of his broad chest. "I hurt you," she whispered, so much self-loathing in her voice that he winced in sympathy. "I never meant to hurt you, James."

He put his arms around her and pulled her closer. "You can't help the way you feel, or in this case don't feel."

She couldn't accept his comfort, not until she'd given him the same honesty he had given her. Pulling back slightly, she looked up at him. "I didn't mean to denigrate your feelings toward me, I just couldn't bring myself to believe in them. There isn't anyone more aware of her shortcomings than I am, and I let my insecurities affect my attitude toward you."

"You've let those insecurities pattern your entire life," he told her shortly. "Don't you think it's time you stopped putting yourself down?"

"It's not that easy when you're an ordinary woman with an average-to-poor figure and a face that's nothing to write home about. I've never been to college or had a stimulating career, or had any particular talents of which to be proud.

"I've always thought of myself as being realistic and practical, but when I met you it was like being caught up in that November storm. You stepped right out of my secret fantasies, more handsome and strong and sensitive than I'd ever imagined a man could be. I felt tossed about and disoriented, and totally, insanely, gloriously out of control. What you make me feel, the way I acted that night, that wasn't me, James. It wasn't me!"

"It was you," he remarked fiercely. "Warm, passionate, giving. All those other things you mentioned are window dressing. When are you going to wake up and see the real person beneath the image of yourself you've created in your mind?"

"I want to," she whispered in a plea for understanding. "But it isn't easy when you've spent twenty years walking in someone else's shadow."

"You were young and malleable when you married, and unfortunate enough to tie yourself to someone who had to dominate your relationship in order to feel like a man. But that doesn't mean you have to pay for one mistake for the rest of your life, Caroline. You have strength, courage and an infinite capacity to love. Those are qualities not everyone is lucky enough to possess, or brave enough to utilize."

Caroline shook her head, and a single tear slipped down her emotion-flushed cheek. "I wish I could see myself through your eyes."

He shifted his hand from her waist, and caught that tiny pearl of moisture with the tip of one finger. "You don't need me as a mirror to your soul. All you need to do is believe in yourself."

Sniffling childishly, she promised, "I'll try."

Laughter began as a low rumble in his chest, but soon broke free of all restraint. When she gave him an indignant glare he swooped down and lifted her off her feet. She loved the beat of his heart against her chest, and the dizziness she felt as he spun her around the room. She loved the tiny lines that radiated in a crinkling fan from the corners of his eyes, and the way his lips curled in a boyish grin. She loved him, she thought suddenly. She loved him!

The realization was terrifying, but Caroline was through running away from the truth. During her marriage she had blinded herself to her husband's weaknesses, blamed herself for her dissatisfaction with their relationship, and carried that burden of failure around with her like a ball and chain. She had been too afraid of letting Frank see the truth, that somewhere along the line she had stopped loving him. She'd been frightened of losing him, frightened of disturbing the even tenor of her days.

It had been easier to live a lie and remain wrapped in the smothering cocoon of Frank's domination. Was it any wonder that he'd searched for a woman who could satisfy his needs, both physical and emotional? She'd tried to be what he wanted, and had nearly destroyed herself in the process. And all because, she thought bitterly, she'd been too cowardly to face a future without the security of marriage.

That was why she'd reacted so adversely to James's proposal, and why she now trembled in his arms. She wasn't intimidated by the thought of loving him, but by the idea of marriage itself. Even now she wanted to hold him, offer him the warmth of devotion and the passion of desire. She wanted to belong to him in all the ways a woman could belong to a man, but that was where the danger to both of them lay.

James was right. She *did* have an infinite capacity for love. It was rising in her now, light, buoyant and joyously enthralling. She was no longer able to resist its seductive appeal. But for his sake as well as her own, she would resist the commitment he wanted from her. She wasn't willing to put their love at risk, because how long would James be satisfied with a clinging, possessive wife? How long could a man with his strong, independent nature tolerate a woman dependent on him for her happiness?

Those doubting shadows were in her eyes as she looked down at him, and James stilled his mad dance around the room. Her lips no longer smiled at him, her laughter had been dispersed like a mist on the wind. Dread clutched at his insides as he slowly lowered her until her feet touched the floor. In a tentative whisper he asked, "Darlin', what's wrong?"

She smiled sadly and raised her hand to cradle his cheek. A muscle in his jaw pulsed against her skin, radiating his tension with the precision of a metronome. "Make love to me," she murmured hoarsely. "I want to feel the magic again, James."

She heard the sharp intake of his breath, and watched the rapidly escalating rise and fall of his chest. But even as his dark eyes blazed with sensuality, he was stepping away from her. "I don't want you to come to me out of some misguided need to make amends," he said, the words grating harshly. "That's not what I want from you, Caroline."

She recoiled as though she'd been struck. "You're still angry with me."

His features gentled, then firmed with resolution. "There are other characteristics of yours I failed to mention," he said dryly. "You have got to be the most literal-minded, exasperating, aggravating woman alive."

Her body tautened in automatic defense. "I'm sorry I no longer meet your exacting standards."

This time she was the one being rejected, and she'd never imagined a human being could suffer such pain and still go on breathing. It was only what she deserved, she thought miserably, but that didn't lessen the anguish or the terrible sense of regret she was experiencing. With dazed incomprehension she searched blindly for her discarded purse, her movements stiff and uncoordinated.

Catching sight of a blur of brown leather through the wavering distortions of the etched glass coffee table, she bent to retrieve it. All she wanted to do was make a quick getaway with as much dignity intact as possible, but the hand James clasped around her wrist made that impossible. His dark brows had peaked in a scowling, inverted V, and the tightness of his mouth denoted a temper barely held in check. "Now what kind of crazy thoughts do you have running around in that beautiful head?"

Tilting her chin pugnaciously, she allowed her own temper to neutralize some of her pain. "You obviously don't want me here, so I'm leaving."

Sudden comprehension caused him to groan, then shake his head in reproval. "There you go again, Caroline. Every damned time I think I'm beginning to see a little light at the end of the tunnel, that inferiority complex of yours goes off like a fire alarm."

"You're the one who said you didn't want me," she snapped indignantly.

"I said nothing of the sort," he denied angrily. "If you weren't so quick to jump to the wrong conclusions, you would have understood the reasons for my reluctance to make love to you."

She shrugged, but the gesture appeared more petulant than uncaring. "What's to understand?"

He emitted a low growl of frustration from between clenched teeth. "I'll tell you what," he exclaimed, his eyes striking sparks off her own. "I should have offered you my support and friendship from the beginning, instead of grabbing what I wanted like a greedy schoolboy.

"When we made love together it was for all the wrong reasons, Caroline. You needed comfort and reassurance that you were still a sensual, attractive woman, and I needed to tie you to me with invisible bonds. Well, I've lived with the result for too long to risk the same thing happening again. This time around we're going to take it slow and easy, and do this thing properly!"

Oddly enough, instead of being relieved by his declaration, Caroline was livid. There he was, standing there all puffed up with righteous indignation, telling her the way it was going to be. Not discussing her wishes, not probing her feelings, but telling her! Giving him her haughtiest stare and most syrupy smile, she paused briefly for dramatic effect. "And if I prefer fast and reckless?"

Observing her mutinous stance through slitted lids, he muttered, "I could shake you until your teeth rattle, do you know that?"

Her chin tilted higher, and her eyes ignited with some of the fire he'd mentioned. Throwing both caution and discrimination to the winds, she yelled, "Be my guest, Mr. Mitchel."

It was the "Mr. Mitchel" that did the damage, and James seemed to explode into movement. Before she had time to utter more than a single yelp, hard fingers

were grasping her shoulders. He was mumbling wonderful, delicious, erotic things into her eagerly recep-
tive ears, and Caroline let herself be manhandled with
a beatific smile on her face.

"You think I don't want you here, you foolish,
stubborn woman?"

His enraged roar was like music, the vibrations a
symphony orchestra keeping time with her thudding
heartbeat. She wanted to respond, but the way he was
yelling, her voice wouldn't stand a chance. Anyway,
she had a pretty good idea that his listening capabili-
ties were nil at the moment. Since her head was already whipping back and forth like a cornstalk in a
hurricane, nodding was also out of the question.

"Shall I tell you all the places I want you?" he continued, letting loose a barrage of extremely descriptive epithets. He jerked her against his hard masculine
frame and pointed to a spot on the carpet in front of
the fireplace. "I want you there, on your knees with
me behind you, inside you, all around you."

His finger stabbed in the opposite direction. "I want
you on that sofa lying down, in the shower standing
up, upstairs in bed on top of me, and floating naked
in the damned hot tub out back." His thundering
voice rattled her teeth with more effectiveness than the
shaking she'd received, but she had no trouble keeping the idiotic smirk on her face. "Hell," he concluded on gasping breaths, "I've even imagined
locking the door to my office and lifting you onto the
corner of my desk."

"I don't think that's possible," Caroline said, breathless. "With both of us sitting up, it would be a little difficult to . . ."

One glance from those threatening eyes had her subsiding meekly, but it couldn't stop the giggles from rippling out of her throat. Soon James's lips began twitching, and a full-throated rumble began to issue from his chest. "Maybe if I feed you I can get you to shut up."

With a teasing grimace he collected her bag and thrust it into her arms. She barely had time to tuck it under her arm before her hand was grabbed, and she was being pulled toward the front door with vigorous enthusiasm. Dragging her feet until she got his attention, she gestured at her casual clothing. "Shouldn't I go home and change?"

His scrutiny was both fiery and thorough, and by the time he lifted his eyes to her face, her knees were acting up again. They almost gave out completely when he replied thickly, "You look delicious."

James saw her shudder on an indrawn breath, and the movement speared heat directly into his groin. He ground his teeth together and fought for control, but when she whispered, "I'm not very hungry," he knew he wasn't out of the woods yet.

"I am," he lied valiantly.

"Since neither of us is dressed up enough for a nice restaurant," she remarked brightly, "why don't I fix us something here?"

He swore her eyes could tempt a saint, and the thoughts scrambling around in his brain were carnal in the extreme. Still, he was going to give sainthood a try, even if it killed him. "We'll eat at McDonald's!"

Ignoring the peremptory tone of his voice, she gave him a slow smile of approval. "Burger King," she corrected with fallacious docility. "I want you to meet my son."

His attention glued to Caroline's mouth, James found it unusually difficult to swallow. She had just bathed the peach-tinted surface with her tongue, her lips were moist and pouting and looked absolutely edible. When she turned to leave, he was so relieved that he nearly thanked her. He managed to follow her through the doorway without falling on his face, but he was a little worried about maneuvering the stairs. His knees were acting up a bit.

Ten

Caroline walked through the doorway with a bemused smile on her face, her mouth completely bare
of artificial coloring. Lip gloss didn't stand a chance
around James. She was still tingling from his good-
night kiss, and her hair was mussed from the fingers
which had speared the silky black strands with a great
deal of masculine enjoyment. James was an extremely tactile man, and she was beginning to realize
just how much she liked being touched.

"Hey, you're home early."

At the sound of Pete's greeting, she sent a fond if
distracted glance in his direction. He was sprawled on
the couch watching television, his long legs draped
over the top of the coffee table. "James had a city

council meeting to attend." She gave a muffled yawn and stretched tiredly. "I opted for dinner and an early night."

"I bet he wasn't pleased about that." He accompanied a knowing grin with a very adult wink. "If James had his way, he'd carry you around with him everywhere. The poor guy's besotted."

She groaned and shoved at his stockinged feet in unspoken reproval. When they dropped to the floor, she filled the space with her purse and the lightweight linen suit jacket that matched her floral skirt. Seating herself with a sigh of pleasure, she curled her legs beneath her hips and turned sideways to look at him. "Might I remind you of what that poor guy has been putting me through lately?"

"Through hoops." The statement was accompanied by an angelic expression that would have done heaven proud, if God could have overlooked the devilish twinkle in Pete's eyes. "It does you good...keeps the old adrenaline flowing."

"And the old feet aching," she muttered with a grimace as she kicked off her shoes. "Not to mention the head."

"Why don't you admit you've been having a terrific time since you started dating James?"

"I've been having a terrific time since I started dating James," she replied obediently. With assumed casualness she added, "You like him a lot, don't you?"

"I like him very much," her son replied with uncharacteristic seriousness. "You've kind of...blossomed lately. He's good for you, Mom."

Although pleased by Pete's growing fondness for James, she didn't want any matchmaking done by her astute son. It was far safer to continue her good-natured grumbling, and she lifted one hand to begin counting on her fingers. "How can you say that?" she asked with an expressive grimace. "Last Friday night we met Linda Avery for dinner in Old Town, and I let the two of them talk me into painting that delightful section of Sacramento red. In the morning the color had bled into my eyeballs, but did he show any sympathy?

"Oh, no, not Mr. No Mercy Mitchel. He still showed up here at eight o'clock and dragged me around Denio's Market for most of the day."

Pete was quick to uphold the reputation of another male. "James cooked dinner for us that night." Patting his stomach contentedly, he slanted her a wicked look from the corner of his eyes. "I haven't eaten that good in months. Cooked cow sure beats chicken noodle soup all to hell."

"Don't swear," she replied automatically around another yawn, "and chicken soup is good for you."

Grinning, he reminded her of how much she'd enjoyed Sunday. "The mosquitoes ate me alive," she retorted.

"But you got a kick out of learning to water-ski."

She laughed and gave him a teasing scowl. "You and James enjoyed it more than I did. Every time I hit the water, the two of you went into hysterics."

"Men do not become hysterical," he replied with exaggerated dignity.

Caroline ignored him and returned to her grievances. She pointed another finger toward the ceiling. "He was an absolute tyrant at work Monday, and then he had the nerve to sit here all evening watching football with you."

"It was a great game."

"Then on Tuesday night we went to that birthday party for Consuelo." She paused and pursed her mouth thoughtfully. "Of course, James really couldn't be blamed for that. Eddie O'Malley and Joe Carruthers spiked the punch."

Pete had just lifted a soda can to his lips, but her tone of sanctimonious forgiveness was too much for his self-control. He inhaled when he should have swallowed, and spit cola down the front of his sleeveless sweatshirt. Wiping a residue of sticky sweetness from his chin, he bellowed with unrestrained amusement. "I've never seen anything funnier in my life. You were three sheets to the wind."

Her eyes flashed a distinct warning. "Any further references to your mother's unfortunate condition that night will not be tolerated, Mr. Barclay. It wasn't my fault the damned punch was spiked."

"Don't swear," he admonished on a chuckle. "You weren't nearly as hilarious as the expression on James's face."

Her eyes narrowed to slits, a worried frown creasing her forehead. Glumly she replied, "He was probably disgusted with me."

"Not a bit of it," he corrected cheerfully. "He looked the way I felt, the night I brought Pammy home two hours after curfew and her father met us at the door."

"Guilty," Caroline guessed accurately. "James tends to be a little overprotective at times, which plays havoc with his conscience."

"I know. We talked a bit after you passed out on the couch."

She glared at him indignantly. "I did not pass out, Peter. I was just a little tired, that's all."

This time it was his turn to nod with sage understanding. "You were so bushed, you never moved a muscle when James stripped you down to your slip and put you to bed."

Caroline's entire body jerked to attention, her mouth flying open in shocked incredulity. "He never!"

Her expression was so outraged that Peter couldn't maintain the deception. With twitching lips he admitted, "No, I'm the one who put you beddie-bye."

Grabbing the throw pillow she'd been leaning against, Caroline bashed him over the head with it. "I take back everything nice I ever said about you."

He presented his can of cola as a peace offering, and Caroline accepted it with a gracious air of forgiveness. Sipping the contents, she asked with feigned nonchalance, "Uh, what did you and James really talk about that night?"

Pete couldn't resist the opportunity to get another rise out of his mother, and gave in to temptation without batting an eyelid. "We discussed the trouble he's having with you."

"Trouble?" she croaked in alarm. "What trouble? There's no trouble."

He gave her his most understanding smile, but his eyes were nervously following the can she was waving in the air. "Yeah, I guess you shouldn't be blamed. After all, it's really his problem."

Caroline gritted her teeth. "James is not having a problem!"

Pete quickly lowered his lashes to shield his expression. If she saw the laughter in his eyes the game would be over, and he hadn't delivered his punch line yet. With a pitying look in her direction he said, "Women don't understand these things."

She gulped and drew in a reviving breath to screech, "Things? What things?"

He rapidly rescued the can from certain crumpling, and with every evidence of enjoyment tilted back his head to drain the contents. "I don't know if I should tell you. It was a man-to-man conversation, you know the kind I mean?"

"I'm going to kill him," she muttered furiously. "I am going to string him up by his heels and get a big stick and..."

Pete jackknifed into a sitting position and wrapped his arms around his middle. Rocking back and forth, he howled until tears came to his eyes.

"You horrible child, I'm going to show you what happens when you tease your mother!"

Before she could do much damage the phone rang. Pete jumped to his feet and gave her an over the shoulder smirk. "Saved by old Alexander Graham."

Caroline rose and started toward her bedroom, but when she turned to wave good-night to Pete she halted in midstride. A feeling of dread prickled along her spine as she noticed the grayish pallor that had crept into his cheeks and the terrifying stillness of his body as he held the phone to his ear.

He replaced the receiver, his movements as slow and careful as those of a very old man. Then he lifted his head and said hoarsely, "That was the hospital calling."

"What's happened?" she whispered.

Caroline couldn't seem to break contact with his eyes, although she recoiled from what she saw in their depths. They were full of a rage and grief too deep to express, too horrible to contemplate. "Dad swallowed a bottle of sleeping pills."

Caroline paced the antiseptic hospital corridor, her hands clenching and unclenching at her sides. She wanted to scream, she wanted to cry, she wanted to break something. And, God forgive her, she wanted to finish the job her ex-husband had botched. How could Frank do this to himself? she wondered furiously. How could he do this to his son?

She and Peter had arrived at the emergency room in a state bordering on shock, each afraid to look at the other. As they questioned the hospital staff, neither dared to voice the fear that was uppermost in their thoughts. It was only after they were assured Frank was going to survive that they were, with a semblance of calmness, able to sort through the evening's happenings.

Apparently Frank and his girlfriend had had one doozy of a fight, which had been loud and violent enough for an alarmed neighbor to call the authorities. According to the police officer who had just finished filling out a report for the hospital records, he had broken into Frank's apartment and discovered him sprawled on the floor in a state of semiconsciousness. And surprisingly enough, Frank had been asking for his ex-wife.

She remembered thinking the whole situation was bordering on the macabre when the doctor joined them at the admission desk. In a clipped, harried manner he had informed them that Frank was no longer in any danger, but would probably be sleeping off the effects of the pills for what was left of the night. "I'd advise you and your son to go home and return in the morning."

Pete had given his head a brief but adamant shake, his manner defensive as he wandered into the nearby visitors' lounge without uttering a word. The doctor had shrugged and departed, obviously too used to the vagaries of human nature to bother arguing the point. Caroline hadn't blamed the doctor, especially since she wasn't in a mood to listen to medical platitudes with any degree of patience. She had been too worried about Pete.

Caroline glanced toward the waiting area where her son was keeping his silent vigil. She hadn't been able to get a single coherent sentence out of him all night, but that wasn't surprising. He had retreated into his own private torture chamber, where no one could follow to ease his guilt. Pete had once told his father he could go straight to hell and stay there for all he cared, and now Frank had apparently done his best to accommodate him. Her stomach lurched sickeningly when she thought of what would have happened to Pete if his father had succeeded in killing himself.

"Mrs. Barclay?"

With a startled gasp Caroline whirled, her pale features pinched and apprehensive as she stared into a pair of sympathetic gray eyes. "Mr. Barclay is awake and asking for you," the young nurse informed her gently. "You and your son can go in to see him now."

"Would it be . . . ?" She cleared her throat of the tightness blocking her vocal cords. "Would it be possible for me to speak to him alone first?"

The other woman nodded, and gestured for Caroline to follow her. "I think that would be best. Your son is taking this very hard, and it might be advisable if he were prepared before he speaks to his father. Mr. Barclay is in a very depressed state of mind at the moment."

Then he can just join the club, Caroline thought, holding on to her anger like a shield as she opened the door to Frank's room. Stiffly she approached the narrow bed, to stand in resentful silence as she studied the wan face propped against the pristine white pillowcase. But the rage that had given her the strength to survive the long, torturous hours of waiting dissolved into nothingness the moment sandy lashes lifted to reveal eyes filled with despair.

The tubes which had been inserted to empty Frank's stomach made it difficult for him to speak above a whisper, but eventually he managed to get the words past his poor, abused throat. "Thank you for coming, Caro."

He sounded lost and pathetic and had aged ten years since Caroline had seen him last. An unexpected surge of pity softened her features as she looked down at him. "No thanks are necessary. In spite of everything that's happened, we once meant a great deal to each other, Frank. As for Peter, he's your own flesh and blood. Where else would we be when you need us?"

His eyes fluttered shut, and he questioned hollowly, "The boy's here?"

"Of course," she replied more sharply than she'd intended. "You're his father and he loves you."

"I don't deserve his love," he muttered. "Just as I didn't deserve yours. God, I've made such a mess of my life, Caro!"

Stunned by his admission, she stared at him in confusion. This wasn't the arrogant, self-assured man she'd always known. Not quite knowing what to say, Caroline placed a comforting hand on his arm. "I'm sorry, Frank."

He expelled his breath on a rasping sigh and opened his eyes. "I should have known you wouldn't take pleasure in seeing me get a little of my own back."

"I'm not the kind of person to bear a grudge."

He shifted into a sitting position against the pillows, his mouth twisted and bitter as he informed her, "After the way I dumped on you, you have every right to hate me."

She shook her head, tiredly brushing her disordered hair from her face. "There have been times when I've hated you, but not for myself."

He lowered his gaze and plucked listlessly at the thin thermal blanket covering him. "You can't hate me any more than I do myself," he said, surprising Caroline. "Did Pete tell you about our phone conversation?"

"Yes."

"He really let me have it with both barrels, but it was only what I deserved."

"Pete was hurt and disillusioned, Frank. It was understandable that he'd fight back." Her eyes filled with tears as she said, "He needs you so much, and you just stepped out of his life as though he no longer existed."

"I know I've never been much of a father," he admitted, his voice filled with self-reproach, "but I do love Pete, Caro. I just didn't realize how much until I'd lost him."

"Then how could you do this to him?"

"Priscilla walked out on me for good, and I guess I went a little crazy."

His body sagged under the weight of Caroline's accusation, while cynicism hardened the outline of his mouth. "I'd sacrificed everything for her . . . you, Peter, my self-respect, and all for nothing. There just didn't seem any reason to go on.''

"No reason?'' she snapped incredulously. "Wasn't your son reason enough? Didn't you realize he'd blame himself for all of this?''

The petulant slant to his mouth was all too familiar, and suddenly any compassion she felt toward him was wiped away by frustration. "Are you willfully blind, or just too stupid to face reality?''

"I never dreamed the boy would blame himself.''

"That's because you haven't really looked at your son in a very long time,'' she retorted coolly. "He's no longer a boy, but a man willing to assume the burdens of adult responsibility. He's alone out there, certain he was the one to push you over the edge. We both know his guilt is misplaced, but it's up to you to tell him that, Frank. I can't do it for you.''

"No, you can't do it for me. Your strength is something I've had to do without, this past year.'' His laugh held a sharp note of poignancy. "It hasn't been easy. I was used to taking you for granted, and it was only when you were no longer there that I realized how much I depended on you. God, I wish I could turn back the clock and start over! Have I blotted my copybook beyond repair, Caro?''

She drew in a startled breath, and her mouth went dry. "What do you mean, Frank?''

"I want to come home.''

Five simple words, but they were enough to shake the foundation of her world. Caroline stared at him in despair as she thought of Peter, and what it would mean to him to have his parents together again. Then she thought of James, and felt as though vicious hands were squeezing the life out of her heart.

Without realizing it, Frank was presenting her with an impossible choice. He was depressed and vulnerable, and was finding it difficult to face the future on his own. She knew his reasoning was, as usual, self-centered, but he wasn't the one she was concerned with. It was her son who had to come first, and his welfare she had to consider. In a desperate attempt to relieve the tension that had arisen between them, she gave her former husband a stilted smile. "You're in no shape to be making decisions like that, Frank."

His eyes sparkled with excitement, and when she tried to step away from him he grabbed her hand between both of his. "We can make our marriage work, I know we can! I promise things will be different between us, and it would make Peter so happy. Please, darling..."

She winced at the endearment, but before she could answer him a voice sounded from the doorway. "No, it wouldn't make me happy, Dad."

Pete moved to stand beside his mother and draped an arm around her shoulders. Looking down at her he whispered, "Because it would make her miserable to be tied to a man she doesn't love, and to one who doesn't love her."

"I do love her. I—"

Pete gave his father a rapier-sharp glance, which succeeded in putting an end to Frank's blustering protests. "You need her the way you always have, but you don't love and never have loved her the way she needs to be loved. I know a man who is willing to give her both, and she'd be a fool to turn him down.''

Caroline saw the simple, beautiful light of truth in her son's eyes and was free. Suddenly, gloriously, her heart was free to soar with the eagles. ''Are you sure, Peter?''

He bent and kissed the whisper from her lips. ''I'm sure James loves you, and fairly certain you love James. You do, don't you?''

''Oh, yes! I love him so much it hurts.''

Frank's plaintive voice interrupted their conversation. ''James? Who the hell is James?''

Pete turned to answer his father's question. ''I've got a feeling he's going to become my stepfather.''

Both Pete and Caroline were unprepared for the bleeding of color from Frank's pinched features, and for the flash of fear in his eyes. ''I'm your father,'' he protested hoarsely, his glance swinging back and forth between them. ''Caro, tell him . . . please, I can't. . . .''

She shook her head, compassion in her gaze for a man who had finally been forced to accept his own shortcomings. He could no longer view himself through the distorted reflection of vanity and ego, because he'd been stripped of both. Frank had always reached out his hand and snatched at what he wanted like a greedy child, but now all the toys were broken and scattered. Through his own selfishness he'd lost everything worthwhile in his life, including his son.

Caroline knew he expected her to smooth things over with Pete, but she was no longer willing to make herself responsible for his failures. Thanks to James, she could finally view her marriage from a different perspective, one that gave her the confidence in herself she'd always lacked. Instead of the mechanical doll she'd always visualized, she now saw a woman who had provided the real stability in her home. That was why it had been so difficult to let go of her life with Frank and to become her own person, she realized with dazed perception.

She'd been relieved of her burden of emotional responsibility for her husband, and her own insecurity had been the direct result of guilt. It hadn't been courage she lacked, only the ruthlessness necessary to break free of the stereotype she'd conformed to for so many years. Now Frank had done it for her, and she wanted to laugh out loud at the gratitude she was feeling toward him at this moment.

The smile she turned on him was confident and self-assured, but her advice was definitely unwelcome. His handsome features darkened into a disbelieving scowl when she said, "Your relationship with Pete is your own business, Frank. It's up to you to tell him how you feel."

As usual, Frank tried to shift responsibility onto Caroline by using her as a diversion. Tilting his chin aggressively, he demanded, "You still haven't answered my question, Caro. Just who is this James character?"

"He is most definitely my business," she replied with an amused chuckle. Glancing up at her son, she asked, "Does my little old matchmaker agree?"

"Go ahead and put the poor guy out of his misery," he replied with a grin. "I'm going to see if I can get Dad checked out of here. We can call a cab to take us back to his place. I'll probably spend a few days with him, if it's all right with you. The two of us are going to have to quit locking horns sooner or later, so we might as well get everything out into the open now."

Pete glanced across at his father. Although his words were still being spoken to Caroline, their content was most definitely aimed at Frank. "He might not be willing to admit it yet," he said softly, "but he needs me, Mom."

Although there was a characteristic trace of petulance in Frank's voice, his response was immediate. "Of course I need you. Your mother might intend marrying again, but you're *my* son!"

Frank's possessiveness caused Pete's entire face to glow, and with a relieved sigh Caroline caressed her son's cheek with trembling fingers. "You're quite a guy, Mr. Barclay."

He swooped her off her feet with an exuberant hug. "That's because I take after my mother."

Caroline burst through James's front door like a whirling dervish, her heart pumping madly as she called out his name. She had stopped at home only long enough to shower and change her crumpled clothing, as much out of vanity as necessity. She was pleased with her choice of attire. Her sole intention was to knock James's socks off. The snug red shorts showed off her tanned legs to perfection, and her flimsy white sleeveless blouse exposed a satisfying amount of cleavage.

He appeared on the landing, obviously just out of the shower himself. His torso was mouth-wateringly bare except for the towel draped around his trim waist, and Caroline stared up at him with hungry eyes. His gaze was just as ravenous as he surveyed her attire. "You must be a mind reader," he said with a laugh. "I was just going to call you and suggest an afternoon drive in the country."

"No, thank you," she declined pleasantly. "I'm not in the mood for a drive."

As she spoke she began climbing the stairs, her green eyes sparkling as she stalked her prey. James watched her glide toward him, the crease of his brow indicating his confusion. "Then I'll take you to lunch and we'll—"

Her curls bobbed as she shook her head. "I'm not in the mood for lunch, James."

"I suppose we can always go—" A low husky laugh interrupted him, which was just as well, he reflected later, since he forgot what he was going to say the moment his gaze rested on the sensual smile curving her mouth.

"Nope," she murmured. "I'm not in the mood for that, either."

"How do you know?" he inquired with a grin of his own. "I haven't made a suggestion yet."

"If it takes us farther than your bed, I'm not in the mood."

His chest heaved as he drew in a ragged breath. "Are you seducing me?" he asked incredulously.

"Do you mind?"

"I'd like to know what momentous occurrence brought this about," he replied carefully.

Caroline knew she could give him a lengthy explanation, but she didn't have the patience at the moment to bother. "Don't you want me?" she asked instead.

James uttered a mild expletive beneath his breath. "That isn't the point."

She cocked her head to one side and began unbuttoning her blouse. "Then what is?"

His avid gaze followed the movement of her fingers, while his own hands curled into the edge of his towel. "You're starting something I'm going to have to finish. Do you know what you're doing to me, woman?"

With a pointed emphasis she slid her eyes down his body. "I have a pretty good idea."

In a single movement Caroline undid the front clasp of her bra, slipping it from her shoulders along with her blouse. James was unable to tear his eyes away from her pink and rose perfection. "You have the most beautiful breasts."

Caroline approached him with the confidence of a woman who knows herself loved as well as desired. "I'm glad you think so."

A hint of amusement twisted one corner of his mouth. "I was hoping you'd need a little convincing."

Her heart in her eyes, she murmured, "It's my turn to do the convincing, James. From the beginning I've shied away from making a commitment to you, because I was afraid of losing myself. But I'm not afraid anymore, my darling. How can I be, when you were the one who taught me to respect myself and my independence?"

"Don't look at me through rose-colored glasses, Caroline. I'm possessive and demanding and I need you too damn much to settle for half measures. I want everything you have to give, and I want you to need the same from me."

Even as he uttered the warning he was reaching for her, drawing her against the warmth of his body with commanding force. With a sigh of satisfaction she accepted his mastery over her senses, while reinforcing her own with clinging hands. "Do you still want to marry a blind, idiotic woman who was too proud to admit that she loved you to distraction?"

His arms tightened around her with exquisite tenderness, and the words he breathed against her shook with emotion. "I think I can handle that."

That wasn't all he planned to handle and stroke and bathe with the moisture from his marauding tongue. Within a heartbeat of time the rest of Caroline's clothing landed on the floor, and James was kneeling like a supplicant at her feet. His hands were busy applying a marvelously rhythmic pressure to her derriere, while his mouth nibbled and sucked at her belly button with languid enjoyment.

Caroline gasped as the tip of his tongue delved into the tiny orifice. "You're not playing fair, Mr. Mitchel."

"You nearly destroyed me with that little striptease of yours," he muttered distractedly. "You're only getting what you deserve."

She cradled his cheeks between her hands and forced up his head with gentle insistence. "I'll never be worthy of this kind of magic, but I promise you I'll never stop trying to be, James."

"Nor will I, darlin'."

With an impatient groan he scooped her up in his arms and carried her toward his large, brass-framed bed. She clung to his neck, her face buried in his throat as he freed one arm to pull back the brown-, rust- and gold-patterned spread. Sunshine spilled through the skylight, bathing the lovers in its radiant embrace.

But the passionate warmth they built together needed no accompaniment. James joined his body to hers, and Caroline was ready to be consumed by its flames. She cried out her fulfillment, and James's eyes burned with the pleasure of his own release. "I love you so much," he murmured.

Caroline sighed and drew him closer, his weight another pleasure to be savored to the fullest. "No more than I love you," she responded gently.

Smiling with drowsy pleasure, she traced the strands of silver hair that mingled with the brown on his head. She felt as though she could float through the skylight and join the fluffy white clouds drifting against the blue sky, but was content to remain where she was. A woman didn't have to soar with the eagles, she thought, not when she was already free to claim her own bit of heaven on earth.

*   *   *   *   *

You'll flip . . . your pages won't!
Read paperbacks *hands-free* with

Book Mate · I

The perfect "mate" for all your romance paperbacks

Traveling • Vacationing • At Work • In Bed • Studying • Cooking • Eating

Perfect size for all standard paperbacks, this wonderful invention makes reading a pure pleasure! Ingenious design holds paperback books OPEN and FLAT so even wind can't ruffle pages – leaves your hands free to do other things. Reinforced, wipe-clean vinyl-covered holder flexes to let you turn pages without undoing the strap . . . supports paperbacks so well, they have the strength of hardcovers!

Pages turn WITHOUT opening the strap.

SEE-THROUGH STRAP

Reinforced back stays flat.

Built in bookmark

BOOK MARK

BACK COVER HOLDING STRIP

10˝ x 7¼˝, opened.
Snaps closed for easy carrying, too

Available now. Send your name, address, and zip code, along with a check or money order for just $5.95 + .75¢ for postage & handling (for a total of $6.70) payable to Reader Service to:

Reader Service
Bookmate Offer
901 Fuhrmann Blvd.
P.O. Box 1396
Buffalo, N.Y. 14269-1396

Offer not available in Canada
*New York and Iowa residents add appropriate sales tax.

BM-G

Coming in July from

Silhouette Desire

ODD MAN OUT #505
by Lass Small

Roberta Lambert is too busy with her job to notice that her new apartment-mate is a strong, desirable man. But Graham Rawlins has ways of getting her undivided attention....

Roberta is one of five fascinating Lambert sisters. She is as enticing as each one of her three sisters, whose stories you have already enjoyed or will want to read:

- Hillary in GOLDILOCKS AND THE BEHR (Desire #437)
- Tate in HIDE AND SEEK (Desire #453)
- Georgina in RED ROVER (Desire #491)

Watch for Book IV of Lass Small's terrific miniseries and read Fredricka's story in TAGGED (Desire #528) coming in October.